Where was her daughter?

Before Julianne could move, the front door of the house flew open and a figure emerged. It was a tall, masculine figure, and her daughter was in his arms. As he moved closer, all sense of reality faded.

Julianne decided this was all a dream. It had to be, because as the moon illuminated the features of the man, Julianne recognized that it was her husband, Sam, who carried Emily.

"I...I thought you might be dead," Julianne whispered, her voice barely audible above the piercing whine of approaching sirens.

"Keep thinking I am," he answered.

Dear Reader,

What's a single FABULOUS FATHER to do when he discovers he has another daughter—a child he never knew about? Why, marry the secretive mom, of course! And that's exactly what he proposes in Moyra Tarling's *Twice a Father*. Don't miss this wonderful story.

This month, two authors celebrate the publication of their twenty-fifth Silhouette books! *A Handy Man To Have Around* is Elizabeth August's twenty-fifth book—and part of her bestselling miniseries, SMYTHESHIRE, MASSACHUSETTS. In this delightful novel, a tall, dark and gorgeous hunk sure proves to be A Handy Man To Have Around when a small-town gal needs big-time help!

Daddy on the Run is Carla Cassidy's twenty-fifth book for Silhouette—and part of her intriguing miniseries THE BAKER BROOD. In this heartwarming tale, a married dad can finally come home—to his waiting wife and daughter.

In Toni Collins's *Willfully Wed*, a sexy private investigator learns who anonymously left a lovely lady a potful of money. But telling the truth could break both their hearts!

Denied his child for years, a single dad wants his son—*and* the woman caring for the boy—in *Substitute Mom* by Maris Soule.

And finally, there's only one thing a bachelor cop with a baby on his hands can do: call for maternal backup in Cara Colter's *Baby in Blue*.

Six wonderful love stories by six talented authors—that's what you'll find this and every month in Silhouette Romance!

Enjoy every one...

Melissa Senate
Senior Editor

Please address questions and book requests to:
Silhouette Reader Service
U.S.: 3010 Walden Ave., P.O. Box 1325, Buffalo, NY 14269
Canadian: P.O. Box 609, Fort Erie, Ont. L2A 5X3

DADDY ON THE RUN

Carla Cassidy

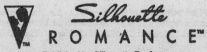

Silhouette
ROMANCE™
Published by Silhouette Books
America's Publisher of Contemporary Romance

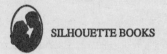

SILHOUETTE BOOKS

ISBN 0-373-19158-8

DADDY ON THE RUN

Copyright © 1996 by Carla Bracale

Printed in U.S.A.

Books by Carla Cassidy

CARLA CASSIDY

had her first Silhouette novel published in September of 1991. *Patchwork Family* was a Silhouette Romance and since that time Carla has written for four of the Silhouette lines.

Daddy On The Run, is Carla's twenty-fifth book for Silhouette. She's looking forward to writing many more books and bringing hours of pleasure to her readers.

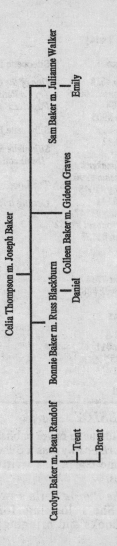

The Baker Brood

Celia Thompson m. Joseph Baker

- Carolyn Baker m. Beau Randolf
  - Trent
  - Brent
- Bonnie Baker m. Russ Blackburn
  - Daniel
- Colleen Baker m. Gideon Graves
- Sam Baker m. Julianne Walker
  - Emily

Chapter One

"Ms. Baker, I feel confident we will be able to place you in a job very quickly." The owner of Martin Employment Opportunities stood and held out his hand.

Julianne Baker rose, her smile wavering slightly as his grasp on her hand lingered a fraction too long. "I appreciate your help, Mr. Martin."

"Bill. Please call me Bill." He smiled widely, displaying a set of teeth too straight, too white to be his own. "As a matter of fact, what I'll do is pull up a list of prospects and bring them by your place this evening."

"Oh, that's very kind of you, but I wouldn't want to bother—"

"No bother," he quickly interjected. "Your house is right on my way home and I pride myself on prompt, personal attention to my clients. I should be by about eight," he said as he walked her to the office door. "I'll see you then."

Julianne nodded and turned to leave. As she stepped outside into the crisp autumn air, she cursed herself for marking the single instead of the married box on the application. Unfortunately there hadn't been a box for "husband missing, marriage in limbo."

It was crazy, but going to the employment agency had been the most difficult thing she'd ever done. She knew it was because it was the first official action she was taking to acknowledge that her husband, Sam, might never come home.

She got into her car and leaned her forehead against the curve of the padded steering wheel, trying to shove thoughts of Sam away.

Sam. His very name brought with it a painful ache and a piercing concern that ate at her soul.

It had been a little over four months since Sam's father had been found murdered in the offices of the family corporation. Sam had been seen running from the building and nobody had claimed to have seen or heard from him since. Four months of wondering if he were dead or alive, four months of doubts and fears.

With a sigh, Julianne started the car and headed for her home in the Hamptons. She'd promised her daughter, Emily, pizza for dinner, which always meant at least two hours spent at Pizza Pizazz so Emily could play in the arcade and watch the mechanical puppet show.

As Julianne thought of her five-year-old daughter, her concern for Sam erupted all over again. Why hadn't he gotten in touch with her? Granted, things had not been wonderful between her and Sam in the months preceding the murder, but she'd never imagined their lives would suddenly be torn apart by such horrible circumstances. She'd thought they would separate, had even contemplated the possibility of a divorce, but she'd never dreamed Sam would disappear from her life as the prime suspect in a murder case.

Wheeling into her long, tree-bedecked driveway, Julianne once again let thoughts of Sam fall away, leaving behind a weary depression and a familiar feeling of desperation.

The house awaiting her was so beautiful, but it had never really felt like a home. It was a status symbol, a fitting place of residence for the eldest Baker heir, bought and paid for by Baker sweat, tears and blood.

Sam had loved the house, but how long could she manage to hold on to it? Sam's assets had been frozen by the police, leaving Julianne and Emily to depend on the mercy of friends and family and the charitable goodwill of Baker Enterprises.

"I need a job," she murmured to herself as she turned off the engine. Even more, she *wanted* a job. She hoped Bill Martin had a long list of prospective employers for her. She had to secure some sort of future for Emily and, in any case, it would be good for her to work again, feel productive again.

"Mommy!" As if conjured from Julianne's thoughts, Emily flew out of the house as Julianne got out of the car. "You're home," she said, launching herself like a little rocket into her mother's arms. "I missed you."

"And I missed you, my little bunny," Julianne replied as she grinned at her daughter. "You're missing a pigtail," she observed. Half of Emily's hair was caught up in a bright pink bow, the other half tumbled around her slender shoulders in dark disarray.

"It fell out when I took my nap, and I wouldn't let Susan fix it," Emily explained as they walked to the house.

"She says I pull." Susan, the nineteen-year-old baby-sitter, greeted Julianne at the door with a friendly smile. "How did your appointment go?"

Julianne shrugged. "All right I suppose." She sank onto the sofa, smiling as Emily scrambled up on her lap. "The owner of the agency is bringing by a list of prospective employers this evening." With deft fingers, she pulled Emily's errant hair back into a rubber band as she spoke.

"That sounds encouraging."

"Hmm, we'll see," Julianne said as she kicked off her high heels. "I don't know how many jobs are available for somebody whose only talent is planning preschool parties and charity dinners."

"That's not true," Susan protested. "You do lots of things really well. You're more organized than anyone I know, and my mom says you're the best at getting people to donate to different causes."

"Yeah, Mommy," Emily chimed in. "And you make the bestest cookies in the whole wide world."

"I make the best cookies in the whole wide world," Julianne corrected her daughter with a smile.

Emily frowned and jumped off her mother's lap. "That's what I said," she replied, making both women laugh.

"It seems to me I promised somebody a trip to Pizza Pizazz tonight, but I can't remember who I promised," Julianne said, frowning thoughtfully as she bent down and put her shoes back on.

"Me, Mommy. You promised me," Emily exclaimed.

"By gosh, I think you're right." Julianne laughed as Emily danced around the room in excitement. "Want to come with us?" she asked Susan.

"Better not," the teenager answered as she walked with Julianne and Emily toward the front door. "I've got a biology test tomorrow and should use the time tonight to study." She smiled. "Maybe next time."

"It's a deal," Julianne agreed.

Waving goodbye, Susan walked down the sidewalk toward her home three houses away. As Julianne watched her go, she thanked her lucky stars that she'd found such a terrific baby-sitter. Susan was the daughter of one of Julianne's close friends. She was bright, energetic, and loved baby-sitting for extra pocket money. Besides, Emily adored Susan, and the feeling was mutual.

"Mom, let's go," Emily called from the car, where she had already buckled herself into the passenger seat in anticipation of the trip to her favorite restaurant.

"Okay. Pizza Pizazz, here we come."

They spent a little over two hours in the pizza place. Julianne sat at one of the tables and watched Emily as she climbed on the plastic jungle-gym equipment, rode the miniature carousel, and played a variety of arcade games. As she ran from game to game, her petite face wreathed in a smile, Julianne inwardly cried for her husband once again.

Where are you, Sam? Why aren't you here with us? You're missing the very best days of Emily's life. Four months. He'd missed more than four months of special moments and growing pains, magical days that were lost forever. Hot tears burned at her eyes, and she blinked rapidly to dispel them. She'd cried enough tears to fill an ocean in the last several months.

She knew her husband well enough to know only the threat of danger could keep him away. Sam would never willingly choose to be so absent from their lives for so long.

She looked at her watch, realizing it was almost seven. Time to get home. Emily's cheeks were flushed pink, a sign of overtiredness, and Bill Martin would be stopping by around eight. Hopefully he would have something for her, a job that paid enough to at least cover their living expenses.

Before she knew it, they were home.

"I had fun," Emily said a few minutes later as Julianne tucked her into bed. "I love Pizza Pizazz."

"I'm glad." Julianne sat on the edge of the bed, smiling down at the little girl who had Sam's dark hair and eyes, his strong chin and full lower lip. "Besides Pizza Pizazz, what else do you love?" she asked.

Emily pretended to think long and hard, a teasing smile curving her lips. "Hmm...you!" She giggled and reached up to hug Julianne around the neck.

"Oh, sweetheart, I love you, too." Julianne kissed her daughter on the impossibly sweet, soft skin of her neck. "Now, you go to sleep." She spied Emily's favorite stuffed bunny on top of the dresser. "Want me to give you Mr. Bunny?"

"No. Daddy will give him to me when he tucks me in."

Julianne's heart constricted as she pushed a strand of Emily's hair away from her forehead. "Sweetheart, you know Daddy isn't here right now."

"I know, Mommy. But Daddy comes down from heaven in the middle of the night to see me. He kisses me right here." She pointed to her cheek.

Julianne frowned, unsure how to handle Emily's latest fantasy. She'd always been a fanciful child, and Julianne knew this new fabrication had found its roots in a little girl's grief over her father's prolonged absence.

"I'll go ahead and give you Mr. Bunny tonight," she said. She got the stuffed animal from the top of the dresser and tucked it next to Emily beneath the blankets, deciding not to confront the issue of Sam tonight. "Good night, sweetpea," she said, then turned off the light and left the room.

Going back downstairs, she looked at her watch and realized it was nearly time for Bill Martin to stop by. She'd been told about his agency by several acquaintances who'd said he was a genius when it came to placing people in positions. It was going to take a genius to find her a job. She'd left college in her third year, without a degree, to marry Sam.

Almost immediately she'd gotten pregnant with Emily, and both she and Sam agreed she would be a full-time wife and mother, at least until Emily started school. Now, with these new circumstances, Julianne was moving up the timetable she and Sam had made together. Hopefully in the next couple of days she would be working again.

Going into the kitchen, she decided to make a small pot of coffee. She wasn't sure whether Bill would stay to go over the list of prospective jobs with her, or just drop it off at the door and be on his way. She hoped it was the latter. It had been a long day and she was exhausted.

The coffee had just finished dripping through the machine when the doorbell rang. At the same moment the grandfather clock at the top of the stairs chimed eight times.

At least he's punctual, she thought as she hurried to the front door. "Mr. Martin, please come in," she greeted him.

"Bill." He shook a finger at her playfully. "I told you to call me Bill." He stepped into the foyer and looked around. "What a beautiful home you have here."

"Thank you." She hesitated awkwardly. "Uh, please...come in." She led him into the living room, indicating the sofa. "Would you like a cup of coffee?" she asked once he'd sat down.

"That would be wonderful." He smiled his perfect smile, a dimple flashing in one cheek. "I missed my afternoon coffee break today, so a shot of caffeine sounds terrific."

Julianne nodded and left the room, returning moments later with a serving tray. Setting it down on the coffee table, she joined him on the sofa as he pulled several sheets of paper out of his briefcase.

"I've gone over your application carefully and noticed when you were going to college you took a lot of child development courses," he said.

Julianne nodded. "At one time I thought I might open my own preschool."

"I have several openings for preschool and nursery school workers." He handed her a sheet of paper with a list of schools and positions available. "There's always an enormous need for good, responsible help in this particular field."

She looked over the list, uncomfortably aware of his dark gaze sweeping over the length of her in a distinctly unprofessional manner. Relief flooded her when his gaze finally went to the coffee mug he held in one hand.

He took a drink of the coffee, then set the mug down and pulled out another paper. "I also made a list of several sales position jobs that are open." He placed the paper on the coffee table.

Julianne leaned forward to get a better look.

"Hmm, you smell good," he said in a tone that was distinctly unprofessional. "What is the name of that luscious perfume?"

Julianne immediately sat back, away from him, irritated with herself for opening the door to allow him in and rankled with him for making her feel uncomfortable. More than anything, she was angry with herself for not seeing this coming, for being too weak to insist he *not* come by the house. She should have known better, should have insisted they conduct business at his office.

She stood with a cool smile. "I'll look over the material you've brought and get back to you if I'm interested in pursuing anything."

He got up slowly, as if reluctant to leave. "There's something I'd definitely be interested in pursuing," he said as he followed her into the foyer. "Why don't you have dinner with me tomorrow night?" He leaned against the front door, making it impossible for her to open it.

"I'm sorry, I'm interested in a job. Nothing more."

"I'll bet you like Italian," he said, his smile distinctly flirtatious. "I know a great little Italian place, makes the best manicotti on Long Island."

"I don't eat Italian," she lied, "and I really think it's time for you to leave."

"Look, all I'm asking for is a nice dinner together, no strings attached." He sidled away from the door, toward her. "You're a very attractive woman, Julianne. I must confess, I'm quite taken with you," he said, flashing his teeth.

Suddenly there was a crash. A vase, which had sat on a small table on the landing above them, came tumbling down at their feet in a hundred pieces. He yelped and jumped back with a startled oath. "What was that? A poltergeist?" he asked as he placed a hand over his heart.

"I don't know," Julianne exclaimed, her own heart battering against the sides of her ribs. "It...it must have been off balance." She threaded fingers through her hair, distracted by the unexpected occurrence.

"That didn't just teeter and fall, it propelled down like it was thrown," he said as his gaze once again sought the landing. He laughed uneasily. "You sure you don't have a disgruntled ghost?"

"Mommy?" Emily's voice drifted down from her bedroom.

"It's okay, Emily," Julianne yelled up the stairs. "Mommy just broke a vase." She turned back to Bill. "I—I need to get a broom and clean up the mess."

"I'll be on my way, then. Let me know if you see anything on those lists that interests you. And perhaps we can discuss a nice Italian dinner another time." Flashing her another of his overbright grins, he turned and left.

Heart still pounding, Julianne quickly closed the door and locked it behind him. Turning around, she frowned at the shards of the broken vase on the floor. How odd. That vase had sat on the landing for as long as they had lived here. What had made it suddenly fall?

As she swept up the pieces she decided she didn't care why it had fallen, she was just grateful it had.

The crash had effectively broken whatever mood Bill Martin had been attempting to set. She shuddered as she remembered the way his gaze had lingered on her breasts, her legs.

She'd been stupid. She should never have agreed for him to stop by her house. "Creep," she muttered as she cleaned up the last of the mess. She would find her own job. There was no way she wanted any other contact with Mr. Slimy Bill Martin.

She went into the kitchen and turned off the coffee maker, then headed upstairs, eager to call it a night and go to bed. As she rechecked all the doors to make certain they were locked, a whisper of worry resurged.

Locking the doors at the end of the day had always been Sam's job. As silly as it seemed, the mere act of having to do that task herself filled her with distress. *Where are you, Sam? Are you safe? Warm? Why haven't you contacted me?* So many questions raced through her mind, questions that had no answers.

Once upon a time she'd believed her destiny was her own to guide, but since Sam's disappearance, everything seemed to be spinning out of her control. Circumstances she couldn't command had changed her life forever, and she was determined to take charge of the areas she could. She was living a life of limbo and uncertainty, but she had vowed to keep things as normal as possible for Emily's sake.

As she got into the king-size bed where she'd slept with Sam since their wedding night, she silently begged for sleep to come swiftly.

It was only in sleep that her love for Sam was allowed to shine through without the complication of other emotions. She could momentarily forget the problems that had plagued their marriage before the night of the crime. She could overlook the little annoying habits he'd had that had driven her crazy. In the sweet arms of slumber, her dreams were filled with the memory of the simple emotion of loving Sam.

Sam Baker leaned against a box of Christmas decorations, a flashlight illuminating the area directly around him. Thankfully the attic was well insulated and the rising heat from the house below kept it a comfortable temperature.

After months of running he was finally home, although home for the past two days had been the dusty, crowded confines of the attic. He'd snuck into the attic while Julianne and Emily had been out of the house, and for most of the past two days he'd only left the attic when he was certain the house was empty, or when he thought Julianne and Emily were sleeping.

He should be thinking of how to solve the mess he was in. Wanted by the police for the murder of his father, certain the real killer was after him, and deathly afraid for his family's well-being, Sam was at the end of his emotional and physical rope. Yes, he should be trying to figure out a way to fix his life and catch a killer, but all he could think of was Julianne and Emily.

His hands closed into fists as he remembered the ineffective wrath that had nearly suffocated him as he'd listened to Bill Martin flirt with Julianne. He'd wanted to charge down the attic stairs, leap over the landing and slug the guy. Instead he had rocketed the vase, then returned to the attic staircase, praying the smashing vase would be enough to send the creep on his way. Thank God it had worked and Sam hadn't needed to do anything more dramatic.

He didn't want Julianne to know he was here because he was afraid the knowledge would put her in danger. He needed time alone to think, time to come up with a viable plan.

Never in his life had he been so bone-weary. Months of looking over his shoulder, trusting nobody, sleeping in alleys and on park benches had taken their toll on him. He'd become an animal, wary and suspicious of everyone, scrambling to stay alive.

At least here he felt safe, he could sleep without fear. He'd even managed a much-needed shower earlier while Julianne and Emily had been out. Wearing clean clothes and a splash of his favorite cologne, he almost felt human again.

There was only one more thing he needed before he would sleep. Looking at his wristwatch, he saw that it was nearing midnight. Surely it would be safe now.

With the stealth of a seasoned burglar, he crept down the attic stairs and opened the door that led to the second-story hallway of the house.

He stood perfectly still for a long moment, listening to the sounds of a house at rest. The tick-tock of the grandfather clock, the hum of the furnace, all the familiar sounds enfolded him and filled him with a sense of welcome.

Turning to the left, he went to Emily's bedroom door. Stepping inside, he was unsurprised to see her still awake, her features visible in the night-light she never slept without.

"Hi, Daddy," she whispered as she sat up. "I knew you'd come. I been waiting for you."

"It's late. You should be asleep." Sam sat down on the edge of her bed, breathing in the scent of her, a wonderful mixture of sunshine and little-girl sweetness no perfume could produce.

"I was waiting for my good-night kiss from you," she announced.

Sam leaned down and kissed her forehead. "Go to sleep now, Emily. It's very late."

"Will you stay with me till I fall asleep?" she asked.

He nodded, and she immediately closed her eyes. He'd never intended for Emily to know he was here, but he hadn't been able to resist sneaking down the night before just to see her while she slept. Unfortunately, she hadn't been sleeping.

When he explained to her that Daddy could only come downstairs in the night, she'd accepted it with a child's innocence. The same way she accepted the existence of a jolly fat man who left toys at Christmas and a giant bunny who left eggs at Easter.

Emily was always filled with stories of fairy princesses and pixies, angels and unicorns. Sam hoped her stories of Daddy were met with the same amused disbelief as the rest of her tales.

Realizing Emily had fallen asleep, he got up from the bed. He started back toward the attic staircase, then hesitated. Just one look. He stared toward the door that led to the master bedroom. Just one look at Julianne before he went back to his self-imposed cell. He needed to look at her face for a single moment.

Before he knew it, he stood in the doorway of his bedroom, his gaze seeking his wife in the tumble of blankets on the bed. A night-light burned in this room, too. A beacon of light in case Emily awakened and stumbled in for a hug.

Knowing he was taking an enormous risk, yet unable to stop his forward motion, he moved to the side of the bed. As usual, she slept curled up on her side, a hand fisted beneath her chin as if she contemplated the dreams spinning in her head.

Her pale blond hair spilled across the pillow like spun silk, and he fisted his hands at his sides, resisting the impulse to touch the soft strands.

Oh, Julianne, his heart sighed its pain. He wanted nothing better than to crawl into the bed next to her, take her in his arms and hold her until morning light broke through the windowpane. Although his heart knew his desire, his head knew the risks. And they were simply too big.

Besides, things hadn't been great between them before he'd had to pull his disappearing act. He had a feeling four months of being gone from her life probably hadn't helped things at all. In fact, the night before the murder of his father, Julianne had told him she was unhappy; perhaps they should consider a separation or think about a divorce. She got her separation, he thought wryly.

Silently he backed out of the room, a slight burning in his eyes as he went back to the attic stairs.

Somehow, some way, he had to fix the trouble he was in, had to find the person responsible for his father's death and his own exile. He had a horrifying feeling that time was running out. Each day that passed, every moment he stayed away, the distance between Julianne and him grew greater.

What he feared more than anything was that when he eventually sorted through the murder of his father and cleared his own name, the only thing left of his marriage would be ashes.

Chapter Two

"Emily, time to get up," Julianne called from the doorway of her daughter's room. She smiled as the little girl burrowed deeper beneath the bright pink blankets. "Come on, sleepyhead. Pancakes in ten minutes."

"Pancakes?" Emily's head popped up at the mention of her favorite breakfast food.

"Yes, and don't forget you have school this morning so dress nice. No jeans." Julianne turned to go downstairs to the kitchen, then paused and breathed in deeply.

Sam. For just a moment she imagined she smelled the spicy scent of his favorite cologne. She closed her eyes, shaken to her core. The scent reminded her of early days in their marriage, when they had spent mornings snuggled beneath blankets, making love frantically one last time before Sam left for work. The memory stole her breath with bittersweetness.

Shaking her head, she continued on down the stairs. Twice since she'd awakened earlier, she'd thought she smelled Sam.

It's amazing what the imagination can do, she thought as she stirred the pancake batter. Smelling Sam's cologne, feeling his very presence in the house. Lately, these kinds of things had kept her sane.

However, it was now time to get busy with reality. She had breakfast to make and Emily to get to school. Despite Sam's absence, she and Emily had to move ahead with life.

A month ago she'd begun taking Emily to a daycare twice a week. When she'd realized she needed to find a job, she'd decided to ease Emily into a preschool slowly to see how she'd adjust. Thankfully, Emily loved her school and Julianne knew when it came time for Emily to go full-time, it wouldn't be a big problem.

The doorbell chimed, interrupting her thoughts. She set the bowl of pancake batter by the stove, then hurried to the door.

"Good morning, my dear." Garrison Fielder greeted her with his usual dashing wink and wide smile. "I was on my way to the office and decided

I needed one last cup of coffee before throwing myself at the mercy of the businessworld.''

Julianne smiled. "This makes twice this week. You'd better be careful, Garrison, or this will become a habit."

"I can't think of any habit I'd rather have," he said as he followed her into the kitchen and poured himself a cup of coffee.

He sat down at the table as Julianne began cooking the pancakes. "Where's my favorite gumdrop?" he asked.

"She should be down here any minute. It's a school day," Julianne said. Her words were met with the sound of little feet pattering down the staircase.

"Uncle Garri," Emily squealed in delight as she entered the kitchen. She ran over to where he sat and, with the agility of a monkey, climbed up into his lap.

Garrison beamed at the child. "You look beautiful this morning, little missy," he said.

"Thank you, it's one of my bestest dresses." She smoothed the ruffled plaid dress primly. "Will you drive me to school?" she asked.

"Emily, you shouldn't impose on Garrison," Julianne chided her daughter.

"Nonsense, I'd be delighted to drive my gumdrop to school," Garrison exclaimed.

"Who's my favorite uncle?" Emily asked, beginning the game they always played.

"I'm sure I don't know," Garrison replied.

"It's Uncle Garri. It's you," Emily laughed.

"And who's my favorite gumdrop?" Garrison continued the game. Julianne listened to their silliness, enjoying the sound of her daughter's giggles.

As Emily ate, she prattled to Garrison, telling him what she'd dreamed the night before, about the trip to Pizza Pizazz, all the things she deemed important in her life.

Garrison listened with a bemused, patient smile, answering her questions and giving her his full, undivided attention.

Julianne watched them as she cleaned up the kitchen, grateful for Garrison's support and affection. Garrison Fielder had been Sam's father's business partner and one of the few people who believed in Sam's innocence. It had been Garrison who had arranged to pay for Julianne's bills when the police froze Sam's assets. Over the past couple of months, he had become a favorite beloved "uncle" to Emily.

He was a big man, with a head full of snowy-white hair and a matching mustache. He looked like a beardless Santa Claus, and Julianne often wondered if that resemblance was what had drawn Emily to him so completely.

"You all right? Need any money?" Garrison asked a few minutes later as he got ready to back out of the driveway. "You know all you need to do is ask."

"No, we're fine," Julianne answered. "I'm looking at jobs and hope to have something very soon. Besides, you've been far too generous already."

His features darkened with a hint of pain. "It's the least I can do for Joseph. Both he and Sam would have wanted you taken care of. I still can't believe he's gone. Every morning I automatically go toward Joseph's office, then remember he isn't there any longer. It's strange with neither Joseph nor Sam there." He cleared his throat. "I'd better get this gumdrop to school." He smiled over at Emily who was buckled in the passenger seat.

"Emily, have a good day and I'll see you after school," Julianne said, then blew her daughter a kiss.

"Bye, Mommy," Emily replied, then waved gaily as they backed out of the driveway.

Julianne lingered on the driveway, reluctant to go back into the empty, lonely house. She should use the time while Emily was in school to do some more job-hunting. One thing was certain, she would not return to the Martin agency. She would find a job for herself, without the complication of fighting off unwanted advances.

Once she was back inside, she decided to spend the day cleaning instead of job-hunting. She sim-

ply felt too fragile to face nameless people reject-
ing her today.

Soon after Emily's birth Sam had offered to hire
a maid to keep the big house clean, but Julianne
had put her foot down and insisted she do it herself. It was one of the few things she did that made
her feel like a wife. Pulling her hair into a ponytail, she changed into a worn pair of sweatpants and
one of Sam's old shirts.

As she buttoned the shirt around her, she closed
her eyes, trying to remember how it felt to have
Sam's arms around her instead of just the cool
fabric of a shirt he hadn't liked. The sad part was,
even before he'd disappeared, the times he'd held
her had been few and far between. Like his father,
Sam had been obsessed with the family business,
leaving little time for anything else in his life.

She opened her eyes, irritated with her maudlin
thoughts. Time to get to work. Julianne's friends
often teased her and told her it was a sin that she
found such comfort in cleaning. But it was true, for
Julianne the task of making beds, wiping down
countertops and running the vacuum was cathar-
tic.

She worked until noon, when the doorbell interrupted her in the middle of dusting the living room.
"Barry," she greeted Sam's best friend at the door
by giving him a quick hug. "What are you doing
here? Why aren't you at work?"

Barry Baxton released her and grinned. "They've changed my schedule all around. I'm now off on Thursdays and Fridays instead of Saturdays and Sundays."

"Well, come on in, I was just about to fix some lunch. If you don't mind tuna salad, you're welcome to stay."

"Tuna sounds good to me." Barry followed her into the kitchen, where he sprawled his tall, thin frame into a kitchen chair. "Bad day?" he asked.

"No worse than most." She looked at him curiously. "Why do you ask?"

He smiled. "I smell pine cleanser and furniture polish. That's always a sign you're having a bad time."

Julianne gave a rueful laugh. "You've known me too long, Barry. You know all my secrets." She got a container of tuna salad out of the refrigerator, then grabbed a loaf of bread. "I woke up this morning and smelled Sam's cologne," she confessed as she made the sandwiches. "I turned over, certain I would find him in bed next to me and that the last four months have really just been a horrible nightmare." She flashed him a lackluster smile. "Then I came fully awake and realized the months without Sam is the true reality."

"Oh, Julianne, I'm sorry," Barry said softly. "I know how hard all this has been on you."

She shrugged and placed a handful of potato chips next to the sandwiches on the plates. "Anyway, it hasn't been a bad day…it's been a bad year. But enough whining from me. How's Miranda feeling?" She placed one plate in front of him, then joined him at the table.

"Pregnant. Morning sickness has hit her pretty hard. She's at that stage where she's miserable and it's all my fault." Barry chomped a potato chip and looked at her curiously. "I don't remember you being so cranky when you were carrying Emily."

Julianne laughed. "You weren't living with me. I can't tell you how many nights I woke up Sam by hitting him over the head with my pillow because he could sleep on his stomach and I couldn't." Her laughter died, replaced by a piercing, bittersweet ache in her heart.

"Speaking of Emily, how's she doing?"

"Emily is terrific. I've started her in a pre-school, and she adores it. She even has a boy-friend, a little boy named Ian who has freckles that dance on his nose when he smiles."

Barry laughed and shook his head ruefully. "Gosh, they grow up so fast, don't they? What-ever happened to her imaginary dragon friend?"

"He disappeared about the same time that Sam did. Since then we've had an invisible frog, a mag-ical headband and a stuffed bunny who only talks when I'm not around."

"Nobody can say she doesn't have an imagina-tion," Barry exclaimed.

Julianne nodded. "But her latest fantasy has me a little concerned."

"What's that?"

"She's started telling me that at night Sam comes down from heaven and kisses her good-night."

Barry took a bite of his sandwich and chewed thoughtfully. "You don't suppose she has seen Sam, do you?"

"Of course not." Julianne sighed. "It's just the wistful thinking of a little girl who misses her daddy."

Barry touched her arm sympathetically. "You know Sam would be in touch with you if it was at all possible."

She nodded. "I know, and that's what scares me so much. Why hasn't he gotten in touch with me? Is he in a hospital someplace, unable to tell anyone his name or where he lives? Or worse? Is he—" She broke off, the unspoken hanging heavy between them.

She flushed and looked at Barry helplessly. "And if he is all right, and he finally returns, how is he going to fix this mess he's in? He's wanted by the police, and I'm so confused about everything." She flushed, having said more than she intended. "We need a change of subject. So, how's work? Garrison stopped by this morning, but he never talks business to me."

Barry shrugged. "It's all right. Everyone misses Mr. Baker and Sam. Things aren't the same without any Bakers there."

Julianne nodded, then smiled as she thought of Sam's sisters. "I still can't believe Carolyn and Bonnie are married and living in Casey's Corners, Kansas, and Colleen just got married a couple of days ago. Now all the Baker brood is married." She steadfastly refused to contemplate if her and Sam's marriage would survive.

"Did you go to Colleen's wedding?" Barry asked.

"No." She frowned. "I had every intention to, even got dressed to go. Then I worried that maybe my presence would remind Colleen of Sam's absence and ruin the special day for her." She didn't tell Barry that the thought of seeing two people so much in love and exchanging vows had been too much for her to handle. Afraid of breaking down in the middle of the ceremony, she'd chosen instead to stay at home, knowing Colleen would understand.

"Well, guess I'd better get out of here." Barry popped the last potato chip from his plate into his mouth, then stood. "Thanks for lunch."

Julianne smiled. "You know you're welcome anytime." She walked him to the front door. "Give Miranda my love."

"I will." He hesitated at the door. "You'll let me know if you hear anything from Sam?"

"You'll be one of the first I'll tell."

He nodded, then with a quick hug, he left. Julianne watched him go, again thanking fate for giving her supportive friends.

Barry had spent the time since Sam had disappeared working from the inside of the company to try to separate fact from fiction and get to the bottom of Joseph Baker's death. As the head of security for Baker Enterprises, Barry had an inside line to gossip and was privy to much of the inner workings of the company.

Julianne knew with certainty that somebody within the company was responsible for Joseph's death. She also knew with certainty that it couldn't possibly be Sam.

Sure, Sam and his father had argued vehemently about the running of Baker Enterprises, their visions of the future at odds with each other. But Sam had loved his father, and Julianne didn't believe under any circumstances her husband would be capable of taking another's life.

So why wasn't he here? Defending himself? Why had he run away instead of remaining here where he belonged? That's the question the police kept asking her, the question that haunted her. As she stood in the lonely, empty silence of the foyer the question that haunted her even more was, if and when Sam eventually returned and cleared his name, would they have a marriage left?

* * *

Smoke. It was the smoke that awoke her. Thick, acrid, it seared the back of her throat and forced hot tears from her stinging eyes. She sat up, nauseous . . . disoriented as she saw the heavy layer of smoke swirl in the moonlight coming through the gauzy curtains at the bedroom window.

Was it a dream? She frowned, rubbing at her eyes, her lungs laboring with each breath she took. What was going on? What was happening?

Fire! Her brain screamed the alarm, but her body refused to acknowledge the urgency. She gasped for air, her chest aching, burning with each drawn breath.

Stumbling from the bed, a single name shot through her, one that pierced through the layer of fog that had momentarily held her inert. Emily! Dear God, she had to get to her daughter.

She groped toward the bedroom door, a frenzied, steady cough stealing most of her breath. She touched the doorknob, nearly sobbing in relief when she felt no heat. Pulling the door open, she gasped as a blanket of thick smoke enveloped her, disorienting her.

The hallway was pitch-black, the air noxious with smoke. Julianne steadied herself against the wall, trying to get her bearings. A burst of racking coughs tumbled her to her knees. She gasped for air and pulled herself back up to her feet, still coughing as her eyes watered copiously. Although she felt no heat, heard no ominous crackle and spark of flames, she knew the smoke was deadly. It burned her lungs and stung her eyes like nothing she'd experienced before.

She fell to her knees, knowing from some past source that the air would be cleaner close to the floor.

"Emily!" she screamed as she inched forward. Again a fit of coughing consumed her, leaving her weak and gasping for good air. "Emily," she croaked.

"I've got her," a male voice cried from out of the blackness ahead. He coughed, his voice muffled as he cried out once again, "Go back...I'll get her out. Go back and get out the window."

Julianne tried to see through the black fog of smoke. Who was it? Who was in her house? A neighbor? Where was Emily?

"Get out!" the deep voice commanded again. "I promise I'll get her."

Sobbing in relief, Julianne staggered back to her bedroom and slammed the door. Thank God. Emily was safe; she would be all right. Somebody must have seen the smoke and called the fire department. They had arrived and broken in to save them.

She stumbled toward the window, threw it open and gulped deeply of the cold night air. At the same time her fingers tore frantically at the screen.

Once the screen had been dislodged, she crawled out, her mind filled with only one thought. Let the fireman get Emily to safety. Please, God, let Emily be all right.

Her bedroom was on the second floor, but there was an overhang directly below her window. As she dropped down she heard sirens in the distance. The sounds of the approaching emergency vehicles disoriented her. Weren't the firemen already here? If they weren't, then who had been in her house? Who had Emily?

Hanging on to the slippery surface of the small area of roof, she peered over the edge, realizing it was a long drop to the ground below.

Taking a deep breath, she scooted her legs over the side and lowered herself until she dangled above the ground. With a scream, she released her hold and plummeted downward. She hit flat on her back, the air painfully whooshing out of her lungs.

Pain. Deep, intense, it tore through her as her mouth opened and closed soundlessly. She didn't realize she was breathing again until she heard her own frantic sobs. She fought against a wave of darkness and struggled to her knees, staring at the house. Where was Emily? *Don't pass out,* she demanded of herself. *Find Emily, then you can let go.* Where was the man who had Emily?

Before she could move, the front door of the house flew open and a figure emerged. It was a tall, masculine figure, and Emily was in his arms. As the figure moved closer, all sense of reality faded.

With the smoke swirling out the open front door like vaporous forms of ghosts in the moonlight and her brain foggy with smoke and fear, Julianne decided this was all a dream. It had to be a dream, she decided, overwhelmed with sensory distortions. It had to be a dream because as the moon illuminated the features of the man, Julianne recognized that it was Sam who carried Emily.

She watched, afraid to move, afraid of waking up if it was a dream, and half crazy with the thought it might not be a dream. Closer and closer he came to where she remained, unmoving. As he came nearer, she expected his features to melt into someone else's. It couldn't be Sam. Could it? Where had he come from? How had he gotten here?

He gently placed Emily on the ground next to her, then straightened.

"I—I thought you might be dead," Julianne whispered, her voice barely audible above the piercing whine of approaching sirens.

"Keep thinking I am," he answered.

Julianne gasped, fighting against the dark edges that crowded into her consciousness. She needed to stay awake, needed to talk to Sam, find out where he'd been. But it was no use. With a tiny sigh, she gave into the blackness and knew no more.

Sam stood in the shadows of the night, hidden from view by a small set of trees at the edge of the house. It wasn't until the ambulance arrived and loaded Julianne and Emily that his heart began to slow to a more normal rhythm.

As the last of the emergency vehicles pulled away, he sank down at the base of a tree, trying to get a handle on the fear that still ripped through him.

When he'd smelled the acrid smoke drifting upward to his attic retreat, sheer terror had riveted through him. As he'd carried Emily to safety, hoping that Julianne had obeyed his command to climb out the window, he'd realized the smoke didn't smell like something burning, rather it held a chemical scent that burned his nostrils and lungs.

He closed his eyes and brought his hands up to cover his face, a vision of Julianne burned into his brain. As he placed Emily beside her, he'd seen that Julianne was dazed, half-conscious. He'd wanted to take her in his arms, hold her close to his heart. He'd wanted to kiss away her fear, squeeze her in an embrace that assured her of safety. But he'd been afraid... afraid to let her know he was really near her, afraid of who might harm her to get to him.

Better that he let her believe she was crazy. Better she believe the smoke had addled her mind, conjuring the image of her missing husband.

He drew his hands into fists and slowly withdrew them from his face. Would this nightmare ever end? Would he ever be with his family again?

Chapter Three

Julianne jerked awake and sat straight up. Fire! The house was on fire. She had to get Emily. She was half out of the bed, then blinked and stared around her. Early morning sunshine streaked through the windows, reflecting off the white walls, the white bed, and the woman in the white uniform opening the window blinds.

A hospital. Immediately the events of the night before returned. Julianne eased back down and closed her eyes, remembering the fire trucks and the ambulance that had brought Emily and herself to the hospital. Emily! She sat back up again.

"Ah, you're awake," the nurse said as she turned away from the window.

"My daughter . . . where is she?"

"When I last peeked in at her she was devouring a breakfast of pancakes and entertaining her little roommate with stories of a singing and dancing leprechaun."

Julianne once again relaxed back onto the bed, aware of a headache pounding at her temples. "So, she's all right?"

"Fit as a fiddle," the nurse replied. "She seems to think being in a hospital is a big adventure."

Yes, that sounded like her daughter, Julianne thought. "When can we get out of here?"

"The doctor should be in here in just a few minutes to speak with you. In the meantime, how about some breakfast?"

Julianne shook her head. "No, I'm really not hungry, although a glass of juice would be nice."

"Orange or apple?"

"Orange."

"I'll be back in a jiffy." The nurse disappeared out of the room, and Julianne closed her eyes. She replayed again those moments just before she'd passed out, trying to make sense from the absurd.

She'd seen Sam. He'd walked out the front door with their daughter in his arms. He'd been leaner, the lines of his face deeper, but it had been Sam.

However, she was certain her faint had only lasted a moment or two, and when she'd regained consciousness fire engines were pulling into the driveway and she and Emily had been alone on the lawn.

Had she hallucinated the specter of her husband? Had it been one of her neighbors she'd mistaken for Sam? Had she somehow gotten to Emily and dragged her outside herself? Had Sam only been a figment of her trauma? It was all so muddied, so confusing, in her mind.

Odd that she remembered all the smoke but had seen no fire, had felt no heat. The entire events of the night were foggy, like a dream barely remembered upon awakening. She thought she'd seen Sam, but that was impossible...as impossible as dense smoke with no flames.

"Julianne?" Garrison peeked into the doorway hesitantly.

"Garrison, come in," she said, relieved to see a familiar face. She sat up straighter, wincing slightly as a harsh tattoo beat at her temples.

"Headache?" he asked, his brow furrowed with worry. She nodded as he pulled up a chair to her bedside. "Yes, the doctor told me you'd probably have a headache. I hope you don't mind, I insisted he tell me how you were the moment I heard you were here in the hospital." He patted her arm reassuringly. "Thank God, you weren't harmed more seriously and Emily seems just fine."

"What about the house? Is it badly burned?"

Garrison looked at her in surprise. "Hasn't anyone told you?"

"Told me what?" Julianne's heart beat the rhythm of dread. Was the house completely gone? Had it burned to the ground? Tears stung her eyes and she blinked rapidly in an attempt to dispel them. Their house. Her home. No use. The tears seeped downward, warm against her cheeks. "Is the house . . . is it gone?"

"Oh, no, my dear." Garrison took one of her hands in his. "The house is fine, without significant damage from what I've been told." He frowned. "Hasn't anyone been in to see you about all this?"

She shook her head, wiping at the tears with her free hand. "The only person I've seen this morning has been a nurse who promised she'd be back in a jiffy with some juice." She frowned, thinking of Garrison's words. "How is it possible there was no damage? There was so much smoke . . . the fire had to be huge."

"There was no fire. Apparently some sort of smoke bomb was set off in your utility room."

Julianne stared at him in disbelief. "Smoke bomb?"

"I'm afraid I don't know any more details than that. If I didn't have friends on the police force and at the fire department, I wouldn't have learned that much."

Julianne wanted to tell him that she'd thought it was Sam who'd carried Emily out of the smoke into safety. But she didn't mention it, afraid he would think she was crazy.

Maybe she *was* crazy. Perhaps the months of stress had finally managed to unhinge the door behind which her lucidity was stored. Like Emily with her imaginary friends and magical animals, Julianne imagined a missing husband acting as a hero. In a child such fantasies were acceptable. In an adult they were evidence of the need for a straitjacket.

"Mommy!" Emily raced into the room and jumped up on the bed and into Julianne's arms. The action and the jostling of the bed made Julianne's head pound even harder, but she ignored the pain, soothed by her daughter's sweetness in her arms.

The house didn't matter, nor did it matter how Emily had gotten out of the smoke-riddled house. Nothing was important other than the fact that they were both safe and sound.

Emily wiggled out of her embrace and sat up. "I have a big bed just like you, and the buttons make it move funny ways. Aunt Letta says I can spend the day with her, and we can make cookies, and she'll teach me how to sew. Can I, huh? Can I?"

"Slow down, honey." Julianne looked at Garrison for confirmation.

He nodded. "Letta thought you could use some time alone, and you know she loves to spend time with Emily. The doctor told me she can be released anytime. And you'll probably be released later this morning."

"Please, Mommy, I love Aunt Letta and Uncle Garri," Emily pleaded.

Julianne smiled and touched her daughter's button nose. "I know you love them." She looked back at Garrison. "If you're sure Letta doesn't mind."

"Mind? It was Letta's idea." Garrison's face softened as he spoke of his wife. "Her greatest regret was that we couldn't have children. Emily fills a void in her life."

"Here we are." The nurse walked in with a glass of juice. Handing Julianne the glass, she looked at Garrison. "Sir, you'll have to leave. The doctor should be in at any moment."

He nodded and stood. "Come on, gumdrop. We'll go back to your room until your mother signs you out." Emily scrambled off the bed and joined him at the door. "We'll be back after the doctor speaks with you. If he releases you immediately I'll be glad to take you home."

"We'll see what the doctor says." Julianne waved and blew a kiss to her daughter. Despite her headache, all she wanted to do was go home. Garrison's words came back to her. A smoke bomb. Why would somebody place a smoke bomb in her house? Who would have done such a thing? One thing was certain, she would never, ever, forget to turn on the security system again.

It was nearly three hours later when she finally left the hospital, taking a taxi to her house. Not only had she had a lengthy discussion with the doctor, who assured her the only ill effect she could expect was a headache, but she was also visited by a police officer.

Garrison had left with Emily, offering to return to the hospital to take Julianne home, but she'd insisted a taxi would be fine. Garrison and his wife had already done more than enough.

She leaned her head back against the taxi seat, grateful the driver was the silent type. The interview with the policeman had been difficult with question after question about Sam, questions she couldn't answer. She knew the police wanted Sam found, and she suspected they thought she knew more than she professed about his whereabouts.

Why a smoke bomb? What was the purpose? Who was responsible? Her life no longer made sense and that frightened her.

She sat up as the driver pulled into her driveway. Although Garrison had told her the house was okay, she was still surprised to see it standing with no significant damage.

Paying the driver, she was grateful her headache had abated somewhat. She was also glad Emily was with Letta and Garrison, giving Julianne an opportunity to spend some time alone. She needed to sort through the fogginess of the night before, try to figure out who had carried Emily out of the

house. Before Emily had left with Garrison, Julianne had questioned her daughter about the fire.
But Emily had been unconscious and had had no
memory of the smoke or of being carried out of the
house.

The police and fire department had spent much
of the previous night and this morning investigat-
ing the house. Julianne had been told that the bomb
had been set off inside a small metal canister on the
floor of her utility room. The police had collected
the canister and debris for evidence. There had been
no clue as to how entry had been made into the
house, and the policeman had warned her that security systems didn't work unless they were acti-
vated.

As the taxi drove off, Julianne unlocked the front
door and went inside. She wrinkled her nose as she
smelled the lingering scent of smoke, and her heart
beat an unsteady rhythm as she remembered those
moments of pure panic when she'd awakened in the
middle of the night and thought the house was on
fire.

She walked into the living room and sank down
onto the sofa. A wave of familiar despair washed
over her. She closed her eyes and covered her face
with her hands.

The events of the night before played and replayed in her mind, along with the thoughts of the
lonely nights, the constant worry since Sam's disappearance. She could still taste the horror that had

filled her up inside when the police had appeared at her door on the night of Joseph's murder. She'd scarcely had time to absorb the fact that her father-in-law had been murdered when she was informed that Sam was the number one suspect in the case.

She knew without a doubt that Sam hadn't killed his own father. The man she married wasn't capable of such a thing. The very idea was ludicrous. But where was he? Why wasn't he here fighting for vindication? She rubbed her forehead, her thoughts disjointed as she shifted through the past.

His absence frightened her, made her wonder if she knew exactly who the man was she had married. In the time of their marriage she'd somehow lost touch of the man, lost touch with her happiness.

"Julianne."

Her breath caught in her throat as she heard the whisper of her name. She pulled her hands down from her face and gasped in shock. "Sam."

He stood in the doorway between the kitchen and the living room and once again Julianne had the disturbing sensation of reality shifting, fading away and slipping out of her reach.

For a long moment she remained seated on the sofa, staring at him, afraid he was an apparition created from her dreams. He was achingly familiar, yet at the same time different. His dark hair had grown longer than she'd ever seen it, and he'd lost weight. His eyes, always so blue, always so clear, appeared darker with tiny lines of strain radiating from the corners. Her husband. Emily's father. Sam. A hauntingly familiar stranger.

In all the time he'd been gone, she hadn't even fantasized what she would do, how she would feel if and when he finally returned. Intense relief that he appeared safe and sound and a strange unexpected discomfort battled with each other.

"Juli." He took a step toward her, as if he was unsure whether she would welcome an embrace.

She shook her head, the use of the nickname he'd always whispered to her when they'd made love caused her heart to resound with a mixture of joy and mourning. She realized she didn't want his embrace, at least not yet. She wanted answers. She wanted explanations. "It was you last night, wasn't it? You carried Emily out of the house," she finally said. "I thought... I was afraid I was losing my mind."

He nodded and eased down into the chair across from where she sat on the sofa. "I thought the place was on fire. Is she all right?"

Julianne nodded, searching his face in bewilderment. "Where were you? How did you get in to get to her?" So many questions fought to be asked. But she wasn't even sure where to begin.

"For the past couple of days I've been staying in the attic."

Again a startled gasp escaped from her. No wonder she'd thought she'd smelled his cologne, felt his presence in the house. He'd been there...just a mere staircase away from her. "And you've been seeing Emily?"

Again he nodded, a whisper of a smile tugging up the corners of his mouth. "She caught me sneaking downstairs the other night." He leaned back in the chair, his gaze remaining fixed on her. Her skin was pale, her eyes still wide with shock, but to him she looked beautiful.

In all the days and nights of running, it had been Julianne's image that had kept him sane. The mental vision of her face had given him the courage to continue, had created his will to survive.

But the expression she wore now was not the one from his dreams. Sam's stomach clenched tightly as he recognized the distance that intensified the darkness of her eyes.

He hadn't known what to expect from her. Anger? Resentment that he'd been gone? "Julianne, I know it's been difficult," he began as he leaned toward her.

"Difficult? Oh, Sam, I've been worried sick." Her voice rang with an edge of unsuppressed hysteria. "Dear God, Sam. You've been gone over four months. I didn't know whether you were dead or alive." She stood and walked over to the window, her posture oddly vulnerable as she faced away from him.

He breathed a sigh of relief, realizing there was no censure in her voice, no anger at all. "I know, but I didn't know what to do. I was afraid of putting you and Emily at risk. I needed time...."

"I knew that would be the only thing to keep you away." She whirled around to face him. "Where have you been? Why have you stayed away for so long?" She bit her bottom lip, a familiar gesture that expressed bewilderment. "My head is whirling with questions. I don't understand any of this."

Sam frowned. There was nothing he wanted more than to take her in his arms, make love to her, lose himself in her, but he knew she wouldn't allow that to happen until her questions had been satisfied. And to answer her questions he would have to relive the whole bloody mess.

"Julianne, please sit down and I'll try to tell you everything you want to know." He waited until she'd sat back down on the sofa, then he raked a hand through his hair and leaned back once again. "You asked me where I've been. Everywhere and nowhere. Beneath bridges, in alleys, anywhere I hoped the police wouldn't find me."

"But why? Why not turn yourself in? You're innocent...."

"And innocent men go to prison every day," Sam replied tersely. "Julianne, somebody killed my father, somebody close to me, within the company. I can't turn myself in until I find out who did it, who killed Dad."

"Sam, talk to the police, let them sort out the crime."

He shook his head. "I can't. I don't know who to trust, who can't be trusted. If I turn myself in they'll throw away the keys, and the real murderer will remain free. The police are looking for a fall guy and I'm him."

"But surely the police—"

"I called the police from a pay phone booth minutes after the murder. I had every intention of telling them exactly what had happened, what my father had thought was going on in the company and why he was murdered. Before I could get off the phone, somebody in a police car drove by and shot at me. I realized then I was strictly on my own."

Again Julianne's bottom lip was caught in her teeth, a frown line creasing her forehead. "What was going on in the company?"

"Dad suspected that large sums of money were being laundered through Baker Enterprises."

"Why didn't he go to the police?" Julianne asked.

"You know that wasn't the way Dad operated. Besides, he knew it would have caused a huge scandal. He was afraid stock prices would drop and the business would be destroyed. He didn't want to go to the police until he knew who was responsible. He thought he could handle it himself." Grief tore at Sam's insides as he remembered the vision of his father dead, slumped over his desk.

Again he fought his need to embrace Julianne, allow her sweet love and warmth to banish the horror of that night and the resulting lonely, frightening nights that had followed. "Julianne." He pushed himself up out of the chair and took a step toward her, then stopped as she held up a hand in protest.

"Don't," she said softly, her brown eyes reflecting her inner turmoil. She sighed deeply and wrapped her arms around herself, as if fighting a chill. "So what's changed since the night of your father's murder? What are you going to do now? Turn yourself in?"

"No, I'm not turning myself in." Instead of sitting back down, Sam began to pace, his thoughts pulled once again to the crime that had not only stolen his father from him, but had stolen a major piece of his own life, as well. "Dad had told me he was closing in on the people responsible for the laundering, and he was keeping notes in a computer file. For several days after the murder, I didn't know what to do, where to go, then I remembered Bob Johnson."

Julianne frowned. "You mean the guy who moved out to Kansas several years ago?"

Sam nodded. "Casey's Corners, Kansas. Bob used to be head of security for the corporation. I knew he had kept in contact with friends in the company and hoped he might know something about what was going on, so I went to Casey's Corners to see him.''

''But he and his wife were killed in a car accident,'' Julianne interjected. ''Did you see either of your sisters while you were there?''

''No, I left soon after Bob's and Mary's deaths. However, before he died, Bob let me use his computer and I managed to tap into the corporation lines. There was a file in Dad's computer I couldn't access, and I think that file holds the clues to his murderer.''

''So what makes you think you can access it now if you couldn't before?''

Sam stopped his pacing and pulled out the charm that hung on a thick gold chain around his neck. ''It's taken me months to figure it out, but I finally realized the computer access code is on the back of the charms Dad gave each of us kids.''

Julianne stood. ''Then what are we waiting for? Let's get to a computer and get that file. Finding out who's responsible for your father's murder seems to be the only way to clear you of the crime.''

''Wait, it's not quite that easy,'' he replied, and she sank back down, her brow wrinkled as she stared up at him. ''A portion of the code is written on each of the charms. All of them are needed to retrieve the computer file. Unfortunately, I only have my charm and Colleen's. Somebody else has Carolyn's and Bonnie's charms.''

"Who?" Julianne asked.

"Somebody who knows the importance of them. Somebody who wants to get into that file as badly as I do."

"So, what are you going to do now?" She stood and once again went to stand by the window.

What are *you* going to do now? Not, what are *we* going to do now? Her words frightened Sam, made him realize that the four months had created an emotional distance between them he hadn't realized. He'd been living on dreams and feeding on fantasies for the whole time he'd been gone, never realizing until now the repercussions of his absence added to the problems they had been having before he disappeared. It had been easy to forget the precarious position their marriage had been in before the murder, but now he was faced with it.

"I don't know," he finally answered truthfully. "I'm hoping if I work at the computer long enough I can break the code without the two missing charms." He looked at her, drinking her in with his eyes. "In any case, it was time to come home, past time. Oh, Julianne, I've missed you."

This time he didn't fight his impulse. He walked over to where she stood. Without pause he pulled her into his arms, burying his face in the sweet scent of her hair, breathing in the fragrance that belonged to her alone.

For a moment he lost his pain, felt sheltered from life's storms. His grief, his fears, the months of running and looking over his shoulder melted away as her body warmth suffused him.

Slowly, reluctantly, he raised his head, aware that she didn't return his embrace but rather seemed to just endure it. For a moment she remained rigid in his arms, then with a small, almost imperceptible moan, she melted against him.

"We should call Garrison and let him know you're here," she said, breaking the embrace all too soon.

"No," he replied quickly. "I don't want anyone to know I'm here. I think somebody suspects already. I think that's why the bomb was set off last night...to smoke me out. But, Julianne, for your own safety, you have to pretend I'm not here, that you don't know where I am. Until I can break that code and get into Dad's file, nobody can know I'm here."

"What about Emily? How can we assure she won't tell anyone you're here in the house?"

Sam smiled. "Everyone close to Emily knows she's given to flights of fancy. She's already seen me and you didn't believe her. I can't imagine that anyone else will."

Julianne closed her eyes and leaned back against the wall. "I don't know what was more frightening, not knowing where you were, what you faced, or having you here and knowing you're still in danger." She opened her eyes and looked at him and he was surprised at the strength that radiated from her gaze. "You know I'll do whatever I can to help you."

"At least I'm home now. I can't tell you how I've longed to be back here with you. Every night I dreamed of being in our bed, holding you in my arms."

"Sam." Her gaze didn't quite meet his and she hesitated a moment, as if dreading what she had to say. "I'd rather you stay in one of the guest rooms for a little while." She raised her chin and he saw a spark of strength he'd never seen before. "Sam, things weren't great before all this happened. Nothing has changed to make it better in the months you've been gone. I—I just need some time...time to adjust."

Sam nodded, trying to ignore the hurt her words created. It had been easy while he'd been on the run to focus only on the memories that brought him happiness, reaffirmed his emotional bond to Julianne. But he hadn't forgotten the fight they'd had the night before the murder, a fight that had been building for months.

No, things hadn't been good between them, and she was right that nothing had changed. But being on the run had reminded him of his love for her, his need for her and he wasn't going to let her go out of his life without a fight. Still, he knew better than to push too hard too soon. She needed time. He would give her time, but he would be damned if he would let their marriage die.

He'd lost his father to murder and his reputation had been tarnished by pending criminal charges, but he could live with these griefs. However, he wasn't at all sure he could stand losing Julianne and Emily. His wife and daughter were all he had left, and the thought of living without them scared him more than he'd been frightened in his months of running.

"Julianne, is it too late for us?" he asked softly.

She sighed, her brow still wrinkled, her expression troubled. "I don't know, Sam. I honestly don't know."

Chapter Four

"Is it too late?"

Sam's words haunted Julianne as she lay in her bed alone that night. She wasn't sure where Sam was, whether he had chosen to sleep in one of the spare rooms down the hall or if he'd decided to go back to his hiding place in the attic.

She knew all she had to do was offer and he'd be beside her, sharing their bed, holding her in his arms. If she'd allowed him into the bed, she knew they would make love and her confusion would only increase.

Just the thought of the possibility of making love with him filled her with a deep yearning. Not just for the physical act of making love, but for the way

Sam used to hold her afterward, their hearts beating mirror rhythms as if perfectly attuned to each other.

But those times were distant memories, gone long before Sam's absence. Somehow in the space of living their everyday life, they'd lost each other, and she simply wasn't sure if they could find their way back to what they'd had in the early days of their marriage.

She turned onto her back, staring at the patterns of light that played on the ceiling from the moonlight wafting in the lacy curtains. The bed was big and lonely, as it had been for such a long time. But she was so confused and her mind was overwhelmed by Sam's sudden reappearance.

For the past four months she had gone to bed every night with a prayer on her lips that Sam would come home safe and sound. And now that he was back, she realized she no longer knew exactly what she wanted from him. Certainly she wanted him to vindicate himself, clear his name from beneath the weight of a pressing murder charge. After that... she just didn't know.

Flipping over onto her side, she willed her thoughts and confusion to go away, seeking the peaceful oblivion of sleep. But her mind refused to turn off. Sam's words echoed in her head, everything he had told her, about why he'd run, how he couldn't trust anyone, and how the only way to clear his name was to crack into the computer file his father had left behind.

Their conversation had been interrupted by Garrison's bringing Emily home. Sam had run back to his hiding place in the attic and he and Julianne hadn't had an opportunity to talk any more. But before the interruption, they'd spoken of the crime, of Sam's sisters and of Emily. The one thing they had danced around was the status quo of their marriage, and what would happen once he managed to clear his name and put that part of the past behind them.

Julianne wished she could assure him, but she couldn't even reassure herself that once they solved the case the two of them would live together happily-ever-after.

Realizing her head was too full for sleep, she swung her legs over the side of the bed and stood. She pulled on a robe and left the bedroom. She checked on Emily, who slept soundly, then went downstairs to the kitchen, hoping a cup of herbal tea would help her relax enough to sleep.

She crossed the foyer and started through the living room, but paused as she saw Sam sitting in the moonlight by the bay window. Although she could have sworn she made no sound, he turned as if he sensed her presence. "Can't sleep?" he asked softly.

"No." She reached out to turn on a lamp.

"Don't," he said, his voice a gentle plea. He turned back and stared out the window. "I prefer the dark." He paused a moment, then added, "It feels safer."

His words, displaying more vulnerability than he'd ever shown, touched her heart in a place it had not been touched in a very long time. She'd been so caught up in her own worry, her own fears, she hadn't fully comprehended the depth of his fear, the nightmares he must have been enduring.

"I'm going to make myself a cup of tea. Would you like one?" she asked.

"No, thanks." He turned and looked at her once again, his pale blue eyes shining almost silver in the moonlight. "But I would like it if you'd bring yours in here and sit with me for a little while."

With a nod, she walked into the kitchen. Guided by the small light above the stove, she filled a cup of water and placed it in the microwave. As the water heated, she got out a tea bag, keeping her thoughts schooled to the task at hand. She didn't want to think about Sam's vulnerability, didn't want to think about what the future held for them.

When the tea was ready, she carried it into the living room and sat on the sofa. She sipped from her cup and watched Sam as he stared out the window. "Are you watching something specific, or just staring at the night?" she finally asked when several minutes had passed.

"A little of both. Although I've learned to enjoy the night, embrace the darkness as a friend." He sighed and left the chair by the window. "I think I've got my days and nights mixed up," he said as he sank next to her on the sofa. "For most of the past couple of months, I did my traveling at night and my sleeping during the day in an attempt to avoid anyone who might recognize me, report where I was. It's going to take a while for my body to readjust to a normal routine."

"As long as you're in hiding I'd say there will be no such thing as a normal routine," she observed. She took another drink of her tea, then set the cup on the coffee table in front of them.

"I've decided to stay in the attic rather than in one of the spare rooms. Emily seems to accept the fact that I visit her at night from heaven. I don't want to make things any more confusing for her by moving into one of the bedrooms."

Julianne frowned. "Are you sure you're comfortable up there?" Guilt played at her heart. He was her husband, and deserved the comfort of his own bed. "You could take our bedroom and I could stay in one of the guest rooms for a little while."

He shook his head, his gaze soft as it lingered on her. "Julianne, I don't want to disrupt things any more than they've already been for you."

Again guilt surged inside her. It wasn't Sam's fault that his father had been murdered and he'd become the prime suspect. "Sam, I'm sorry that I can't just pretend things are back to normal...."

"Shh." He placed an arm around her shoulders and, after a moment of hesitation, she sank against the warmth of his side. "I know it was a shock, seeing me standing here this afternoon. I'd be unrealistic if I expected things to magically be all right after being gone for so long."

With one hand he reached up and stroked the length of her hair, and she felt the tension slowly ebb from his body as he continued the stroking motion. "We'll take this mess one day at a time, Julianne. I'll crack into that computer file and clear my name. The police will arrest my father's killers, then we'll be free to go back to the life we had before this nightmare began."

Julianne closed her eyes and drew in a deep breath, knowing now was not the time to tell him that she didn't want the life they'd had. Instead she cuddled closer against him, enjoying the familiar, comforting scent of him. He was home. For now it was enough. Later she would decide if she wanted him to stay.

Sam leaned back against the sofa, his hand still caressing the silk of her hair. For the first time in months he felt safe, at peace. With her wonderful scent surrounding him and the warmth of her body against his, he felt the last of the tension ebb from inside him.

He could tell the moment she fell asleep, when her body finally relaxed completely and molded itself against his side. In sleep, she accepted him completely, leaving behind the slight reservation that had kept her unyielding while awake. It was a sweet surrender, and he tightened his arm around her, wanting to erase any lingering memory of all the lonely nights they'd suffered while apart.

He wasn't sure if he'd made a mistake in not letting her know he was here. When he'd awakened with the smoke swirling in the house, filling the upstairs with noxious fumes, his only thought had been to save his family. Even after carrying Emily out of the house, he had been able to tell by the look in Julianne's eyes that she was in shock.

He could have disappeared again and allowed her to think she'd dreamed his presence, hallucinated his rescue. It would have been easier that way for her.

However, when he'd seen her standing in the living room that afternoon, looking so lost, so vulnerable, he knew he couldn't stay hidden another moment.

The smoke bomb worried him. Somebody suspected he was here, hiding out in the house. That could be the only reason to set off such a device. Had somebody stood in the dark shadows of the night and watched him carry his child to safety? The thought chilled him. He could only hope that

Julianne was the only person who saw him emerge from the house.

As he remained in the darkness of the room, holding his wife, his thoughts turned to the Baker corporation. Baker Enterprises. His father's life-blood. It had probably gone to hell in a handbasket since he'd been gone. Garrison Fielder was an adequate administrator, but he had no vision, no imagination, when it came to growth and expansion. Sam's sister Carolyn had been a valuable asset to the company, but she'd quit her job soon after their father's murder to move to Casey's Corners, Kansas, and adopt the Johnson twins. Bob and Mary Johnson had been friends of Carolyn's, had even named Sam's sister as godmother of their twin boys. A tragic car accident had taken Bob's and Mary's lives, and Carolyn had gone to Casey's Corners to see to the twins' welfare.

He missed his sisters. Carolyn, Bonnie, and Colleen. The four of them had endured growing up without a mother and with a workaholic father. They'd survived being separated and sent to various boarding and prep schools, but there had always been a special bond between them physical distance couldn't destroy.

The one good thing that had come from the murder and Sam's disappearance, was that in the time he'd been gone, each of his sisters had found love and married. Carolyn had wed the godfather of the twins who'd been left parentless by a car accident. Bonnie had married a deputy sheriff with a young son, and was now pregnant. And just last week Colleen had wed Gideon Graves, a private investigator she'd hired to find Sam.

Gideon and Sam had met the night Sam snuck through Colleen's bedroom window to "borrow" her charm necklace. Gideon had spied him and wrestled him to the ground. It had taken some fast talking, and Colleen's pleas, for Gideon to finally agree to help Sam instead of turn him over to the police.

Sam dragged a hand down his face, exhaustion blurring his thoughts. He was glad his sisters had found happiness in the aftermath of all the horror. It was important to him that something good had come out of the mess his own life had become.

He had to find out who had killed his father. He had to discover who was using the company for nefarious purposes. Baker Enterprises was Sam's legacy from his father, the final piece of his heritage he had to hang on to. He had to crack that computer file. He had to clear his name and save the company.

Once that was behind him, he could exert all his energies, the rest of his life, making up to Julianne for the past lost months.

He closed his eyes. Of course Julianne had reservations about him, about their future. He was still a wanted man, a fugitive from justice.

She stirred against him, a small moan escaping her lips, and he wondered if she experienced the same kind of nightmares that haunted him. He sighed, realizing he couldn't even begin to guess what she dreamed. There had been a time he was sure he could read her mind, knew her dreams before she had them. But in the brief time they'd spent together this afternoon and evening, he hadn't been sure of her thoughts, hadn't had a clue as to what was going on in her mind. He wondered when he'd stopped knowing her. When things had changed between them . . .

Although she was right here next to him, so close against his heart, the emotional distance between them was miles. With a heavy sigh he closed his eyes, for the moment willing to accept what Julianne offered. Just holding her in his arms would have to be enough for now.

Julianne awoke to the golden hues of the early morning sun streaming through the window and one of her arms sound asleep. Somehow in the course of the night they had shifted positions while sleeping, resulting in her arm being trapped beneath his back.

Gently disentangling herself, she sat up, her gaze lingering on Sam. In sleep, the lines of strain that had radiated from his eyes were relaxed, making him appear younger than his thirty-six years. She remembered the first time she'd met him, when he'd come to her college to give a business seminar.

She could still remember the thrill of sitting in the front row and that single moment when his gaze had connected with hers. Across the expanse of stage, brighter than the spotlights that played on his features, it was a connection that exploded in her heart, and she knew at that moment she would be seeing more of this man.

Sure enough, at the cocktail party immediately following the seminar, he found her and before the evening was over, Julianne was in love. Sam was the most dynamic, exciting man she'd ever known. She was enchanted by his charm, bewitched by his wit, and in awe of his confidence and apparent emotional strength. He was a man who didn't seem to need anyone, but who made it clear he wanted her in his life.

They were married three months later and Julianne quickly learned she had not only gained a husband, but a corporation, as well. The family business was as much a part of Sam as his azure eyes and the small mole on the side of his neck.

With the golden hues of dawn painting his sleeping features, a wistful bittersweet longing rose up inside her. It was the memory of love so pure, so clean, it ached within. When had loving Sam become so difficult? Where once she couldn't imagine living life without him, she now wasn't sure she could go back to living with him.

Unsettled by her thoughts, tasting the bitterness of forgotten dreams and unfulfilled hopes, she got up from the sofa and quietly made her way to her bedroom upstairs.

It took her only a few minutes to shower and dress for the day. When she left the bedroom and started down the stairs, the scent of fresh coffee greeted her, letting her know Sam had awakened.

When she entered the kitchen he grabbed a second cup from the cabinet. "Good morning," he said, gesturing her to sit down at the table.

"Thanks," she murmured as he set a cup of coffee in front of her, then poured one for himself and joined her.

Sam smiled at her. "Been a long time since I shared my first cup of coffee in the morning with my wife."

Julianne nodded, trying to remember the last time she and Sam had begun a morning together. It had been long before Joseph's murder, way before Sam's disappearance. "If I remember correctly, the last time we had coffee together in the morning was when Emily was still a baby."

"No, surely not," Sam said in disbelief.

"It was when Emily was about six months old that you started going into the office so early in the mornings." It was also about that same time he began working late into the evenings.

"Dad was a slave driver," he said, then took a sip of his coffee. Julianne didn't say anything, although she knew the truth was that Joseph Baker had been a workaholic and Sam was cut from the same bolt of cloth. He set his cup down, then looked at her curiously. "Tell me, why on earth was that man here the other night talking to you about jobs?"

Julianne frowned. "You mean Bill Martin?" Her eyes widened in realization. "It was you, wasn't it? You made that vase fall from the landing."

Sam nodded. "The worm was lucky I didn't make his teeth fall out of his head."

"Oh, Sam, you should have seen his face." She threw back her head and laughed. "He went from smooth to scared in a split second. And his fake teeth almost did fall right out of his head."

He grinned, responding to the sound of her low, musical laughter. He'd always loved the richness of her laugh, had spent the months of their courtship making her do so as often as possible.

His smile faded and he reached out and stroked the back of one of her hands. "I love to hear you laugh. We haven't had many reasons to laugh lately, have we?"

She shook her head and wiped a strand of her shining gold hair behind an ear. "No, we haven't."

They fell silent, and again Sam wished he could read her mind, what thoughts scurried around in her head. There was a distance in her eyes he couldn't seem to breach. Time, he reminded himself. She needed time.

"You asked me why Bill Martin was here," she said, breaking the silence. "Sam, all our assets have been frozen by the police. If not for Garrison, I don't know what we'd have done. He's been paying the bills, giving me money to live on."

A renewed despair clawed its way through Sam as he realized that while he was gone, Julianne and Emily had been dependent on others for their very livelihood. The crime of his father's murder had robbed him of his pride as a man supporting his family.

He raked a hand through his hair. "I didn't even think about that. I knew better than to try to access any of the accounts or use a charge card, knowing it would leave a paper trail, but I didn't dream you wouldn't be able to get to any of the funds."

"Both Garrison and Barry have been wonderfully supportive," she said. "And in any case, I'm going to get a job."

"But that's not necessary now. If you can just hang on a little while longer we'll sort this mess out and things will go back to the way they were," he replied.

Julianne shook her head. "It doesn't matter. Even after we get all this straightened out, I've decided I want a job."

Again Sam saw a steely strength in her eyes, one he'd never seen before his absence. He realized the past months of stress and strain had changed not only him, but Julianne, as well. In all the time of being on the run, the one thought that had sustained him was that eventually he would be vindicated and everything in his life would go back to normal.

But as he looked at his wife's face, felt the emotional restraint emanating from her, he wondered if it would be possible to go back.

"Daddy!"

Sam turned at the sound of his daughter's squeal, laughing in delight as she catapulted into his lap. "What are you doing up so early?" he asked as he cuddled her little-girl sweetness close.

"I woke up and heard your voice. I didn't know you could come out in the daytime." Her blue eyes studied him in delight. "You're my ghost daddy and I thought ghosts only came out at night."

Sam exchanged a look with Julianne, unsure how to handle this development. Before he had a chance to reply, Emily scrambled off his lap and requested pancakes for breakfast.

"One of these days you're going to eat so many pancakes you'll turn into one," Julianne said as she stood and went to the cabinet where the pancake mix was kept.

Emily crawled back up on Sam's lap, her body still maintaining the residual warmth of sleep. "Daddy, will you stay and eat pancakes with us?" she asked.

"I think I could manage to eat a couple," he agreed.

As Julianne prepared the pancakes, Sam set the table and Emily filled the early morning with her childish chatter. She talked about school and her new boyfriend, Ian. "He's nice," she explained. "He always shares his cookie with me during treat time. If it's the chocolate cookies I tell him no-thank-you 'cause I know those are his favorites."

"That's very thoughtful of you," Sam replied.

"But when it's the lemon cookies, I always say yes...'cause those are my favorites," Emily added, and Julianne and Sam laughed.

Breakfast was pleasant, with Emily diverting Sam's attention from his problems. Even Julianne seemed to relax and let down her guard. Her eyes sparkled the way Sam remembered them and her smile seemed less forced when she gazed at him. Hope buoyed his heart, to be immediately squashed as the doorbell rang.

Sam jumped up from the table as he and Julianne exchanged a panicked gaze. "Emily, why don't you go upstairs and get dressed and pick up your room?" Julianne said as she whisked Sam's plate and cup off the table and into the dishwasher.

"Wanna come and help me, Daddy?" Emily asked.

"Emily, Daddy has to go now. Somebody is at the door and..."

"I know, nobody can see my ghost daddy except Mommy and me," Emily said as if it were the most natural thing in the world.

"Something like that," Sam replied.

"Go," Julianne said both to her daughter and her husband as the doorbell rang again.

As Sam raced up to his hiding place in the attic, a renewed sense of urgency filled him as the expression on Julianne's face burned in his heart.

For just a few moments they had been a normal family eating breakfast and enjoying each other's company. With the ring of the doorbell, the truth of their situation had intruded, shattering the normalcy. Julianne's features had grown taut, her eyes filled with helplessness and an undirected anger. Undirected because she didn't know who to blame. Neither did Sam.

He slumped against the Christmas ornament box and covered his face with his hands. Time was running out . . . sand filtering through an hourglass at a rate he couldn't stem. He had to clear his name, had to find out who killed his father, and he had to do it as soon as possible. His biggest fear was that if he took too long and the sand ran out, Julianne would be gone.

Chapter Five

Julianne's heart thudded anxiously as she went to answer the door. She was relieved to see Barry instead of a policeman with a search warrant.

"Julianne, I was at work and heard about the smoke bomb. Are you all right? Is Emily okay?"

She smiled at Barry's outburst of concern. "We're fine. The only damage was a scorch mark on the floor of my utility room." She hesitated, knowing he would think it odd if she didn't invite him in for a cup of coffee and yet her mind whirled, wondering if she'd hidden all evidence of Sam's presence. "Coffee?" she finally asked.

He shook his head. "No, I've got to get back to work, I just wanted to stop by and make sure you and Emily were okay. I completely lost it when I heard about the bomb and that you'd both been taken to the hospital.''

"It was frightening," she admitted.

Barry gave her a quick hug. "Do they have any clues? Do the police have any idea who's responsible? Why somebody would do something like that? Jeez, a smoke bomb."

"No. At least, they haven't told me anything," Julianne replied.

"Thank God, you and Emily are all right, that's the important thing." He backed down the porch steps. "I'll have Miranda give you a call tonight. She's been wanting to get the two of you over for dinner. Maybe we can do it next week."

"That sounds great," Julianne agreed. "Barry, thanks for stopping by," she added as he paused at his car door.

"I worry about you and the munchkin. Besides, Sam's one of my best friends. If I can't worry about his wife in his absence, who can?" He gave her a jaunty salute, then turned and got into his car.

Julianne closed the door and leaned against it for a moment. She knew how upset Barry had been about Sam, and she felt guilty for not telling him that Sam was safe and sound, tucked away beneath the eaves of the house.

She turned around as Sam came creeping down the stairs. "It was Barry. He'd heard about the smoke bomb and wanted to make sure Emily and I were all right.''

Sam nodded and sank down on the bottom step of the staircase. ''How are he and Miranda doing?''

''They're doing terrific. Miranda is pregnant and suffering the dreaded morning sickness,'' she answered.

His jaw dropped in astonishment. ''Last I heard they had decided to wait a couple of years before having kids.''

''You've been gone a long time, Sam. Miranda didn't want to tell anyone until she was three months along. Besides, things change, people change.''

His gaze held hers, intense and probing, as if he sought to look into her soul, see the changes that had taken place in her.

She broke the eye contact, instead focusing on Emily who had come down the stairs. ''Did you clean your room?'' she asked the little girl.

Emily nodded. ''And I even made my bed,'' she announced proudly. She looped an arm around Sam's neck. ''Daddy, wanna come and play house with me? We could have a tea party.''

Sam pulled her close to him and kissed her cheek. ''I'll make a deal with you. I've got some work to do this morning, but when I take a break for lunch I'd be delighted to have a tea party with you.''

"Oh, goody." Emily clapped her hands together in excitement. "I'm gonna invite all my favorite stuffed animals." She looked at Julianne. "And you can come, too, Mommy."

"It sounds wonderful," Julianne replied. Oh, what she wouldn't give to be able to feel the same undiluted joy, the same unadulterated acceptance Emily obviously felt in having Sam back home. What she wouldn't give to shed the doubts, the uncertainty of the future.

"I'm gonna go set my table." Like a miniature tornado, Emily whirled around and bounced back up the stairs toward her room.

Sam smiled at Julianne. "She's quite a kid."

"Yes, she is," Julianne agreed. "I'm sorry you've missed four months of her growth."

He winced. "So am I." He pushed himself up off the stair step. "I know it's going to be difficult keeping my presence here a secret. I know how much you hate lying."

"Sam, if it assured your safety, I'd lie to my own mother."

"Whew, I'm not sure I'd have the guts to lie to your mother." He shot her a grin, one reminiscent of the happier moments of their life together.

"Mom loves to think she intimidates you."

"She does intimidate me," Sam insisted, although his eyes sparkled with obvious affection. "She doing okay?"

Julianne nodded. "She's fine. She calls once a week to check up on us and see if there's been any word from you."

Sam's features tightened bleakly. "What a nightmare," he said softly. "I never realized all the people I'd affected, all the loved ones I'd hurt when I took off. I just knew I had to get away, stay away from you and Emily so nobody would try to get to me through you. I still pray nobody tries to harm you to get to me. I don't want you to be in danger because of me."

He looked so lost, so forlorn, that Julianne's heart ached for him. She stepped closer and placed a hand on his shoulder. His muscle tensed beneath her touch and she remembered how she loved gripping his broad shoulders when they made love, feeling the play of his muscles beneath the smoothness of his skin. How she had missed making love to Sam. She shoved this memory away, not wanting the months of deprivation to muddle her thoughts.

Besides, she knew making love with Sam wouldn't solve anything, wouldn't make her forget how unhappy she had been with their marriage before he'd disappeared. "We'll get through this, Sam. Somehow, some way we'll sort all this out and go on."

He seemed to hold his breath, his gaze once again delving into hers. She could almost hear the question in his eyes. Would they be together when this was all straightened out? Would they remain married or would they take up separate lives?

She dropped her hand and stepped away before he could actually voice his concerns, ask the questions she simply couldn't answer. "I need to finish putting away the breakfast dishes," she said.

Raking a hand through his hair, he followed her toward the kitchen. "I'll grab a cup of coffee and the laptop computer and head back up to the attic. I've got to get busy trying to crack open that file."

"Why don't you just use the computer in the den?" she asked.

"If somebody comes to the door, I'll be trapped in the den. I'd feel better working up in the attic where nobody can surprise me." He poured a cup of coffee. "What are your plans for the day?"

"I'm not sure. I'm going to check out the Want Ads in the morning paper, then clean out a couple of closets. The corporation is working on their annual winter charity drive and needs clothing. Emily has so many things she's outgrown, and I'm sure there are things I don't wear anymore."

"If I get wound up in this work and don't surface by noon, would you call up to me when Emily is ready for the tea party?" he asked.

"No problem," she agreed. When he left the kitchen, Julianne felt a modicum of tension leave her. She poured herself a cup of coffee and sat down at the kitchen table.

She knew Sam needed her to assure him of her support, that he wanted her to tell him when this was all over and his name was cleared they would still be together as a family. But how could she assure him of something she wasn't sure of herself?

There was a part of her heart that would always love Sam. He was the father of her child, the man she had pledged her love to before family and God. However, in the last few years, he had also become the thief of her dreams.

She sipped her coffee, her heart and mind in turmoil. How could she tell him about her own unhappiness, of her fears of stepping back into the role she'd played in his life before the murder?

She'd been miserable. She'd tried to tell him before but he'd been unwilling to listen. Had he forgotten the fight they'd had the night before his father's murder? Or had he ignored her even when she'd cried and tried to talk to him about their problems?

Still, how could she burden him with all of her own unhappiness now, when he was fighting for his very life in a dangerous game where there were no rules?

She couldn't. She couldn't add to his burden. The only thing she could do was support him as best she could until he figured everything out.

He needed her now, and she couldn't turn away from that. Sam needing her was so novel, intensely evocative and a temporary thing. It would be easy to be seduced by it, bewitched into believing herself necessary to his very existence. But she knew better. She knew that Sam had never really needed anything but the Baker corporation. She couldn't compete with the family business, didn't know how to compete.

And the worse thing he could have done was to disappear for all those months and allow her to realize she actually could survive without him.

Sam rubbed his eyes then massaged the back of his neck. Looking at his watch he realized it was nearly eleven. He'd been working at the computer nonstop for nearly three hours but hated to quit even though he needed to stretch.

There had to be a way to get into his father's program. The phoenix file. He grabbed the charm hanging around his neck, fingering the heavy gold image of the mythical bird.

He'd thought it odd at the time his father had given it to him. Joseph Baker rarely bought gifts for his children, especially something as frivolous as a gold necklace. He should have known it was more than just a necklace... how like his father to conceal the code to an important file on the back of the charms.

Sam's hand tightened around the piece of jewelry. If only he'd figured it out sooner. If only he'd been able to get Carolyn's and Bonnie's charms before somebody else had stolen them. With only two of the charms, he had half a code and a million possible combinations of numbers before he hit on the correct one.

He leaned his head back and closed his eyes, for a moment he was overwhelmed by the odds of success. How long would it take him before he eventually hit upon the correct code? A mental vision of himself years from now filled his head. His hair gray, with a Rip Van Winkle beard, he would be a hermit hidden away in the attic still seeking to clear his name.

Swallowing hard, he shoved such thoughts away. Failure wasn't in his blood. Nor was giving up. He was a Baker, a fighter, and he wasn't about to be beaten by a faceless, nameless enemy who was using the company for ill-gain.

With renewed energy, he went back to work, punching in numbers, seeking the magical combination that would open the file to give him back his life.

"Sam?"

Julianne's voice pulled him from the computer screen. He shut off the computer and went to the stairs where she stood at the bottom. "The tea party is about to begin," she said.

He set aside the computer and flew down the stairs, eager to spend some time with his two most favorite women.

"The simple tea party has transformed into an elegant luncheon," she said as he reached the bottom of the stairs. "Emily has decorated the room and insisted I fix fancy finger sandwiches and use our best crystal glasses."

"Give me ten minutes," Sam said as he headed toward their bedroom. "I want to wash up a little for this extravaganza."

Standing beneath the hot spray of the shower, Sam was looking forward to Emily's tea party. He frowned, trying to remember the last time he'd spent a fun afternoon with Emily and Julianne.

He couldn't remember. Before that fateful night, there had always been too much work, too little time. He intended to change that starting right now.

Out of the shower, he stood in the walk-in closet, trying to decide what to wear for a special tea party. Decision made, he dressed quickly, then headed for Emily's room.

"Oh, Daddy." Emily clapped her hands together in delight when he walked in. "You look so handsome."

Sam grinned, smoothing down his tuxedo jacket. "This seemed like a dress up kind of affair."

Emily eyed Julianne in her jeans and sweatshirt. "Mommy, you aren't right for a 'fair. You need to put on a pretty party dress."

Julianne started to protest, but one look at Emily's face changed her mind. The little girl positively vibrated with excitement and what could be more exciting than having Mom and Dad play dress up for a special tea party? "Okay, I'll be right back," she said as she left the bedroom.

This is crazy, she thought a few minutes later as she slipped into a pale peach cocktail gown. She was dressing for a tea party where the guest of honor was a man wanted for murder and the other attendees were stuffed animals and imaginary friends belonging to a five-year-old.

She should be job-hunting. She should be soul-searching. She should be deciding what she wanted for her future. And instead she was preparing for a Mad Hatter kind of tea party.

Sliding into the matching high heels, she gave herself a cursory glance in the mirror. She'd lost weight since Sam's disappearance. The months of strain and worry showed in the shadows beneath her eyes, the tiny lines that wrinkled her brow. She thought about putting on some makeup, then dismissed the idea. She smoothed a strand of her hair, then turned and went back into Emily's bedroom.

"Now it's a real tea party," Emily said, dancing in delight around her mother and father. She grabbed them each by the hand and tugged them over to the miniature table and chairs. "Now, Mommy, you sit here," she instructed, pointing to one of the little wooden chairs. "And, Daddy, you sit right here next to her."

As Julianne and Sam were seated, Emily arranged chairs for Leonard the Lion, Wally Walrus and a remaining chair for the mysterious, invisible Mr. Leprechaun.

Emily served with perfect hostess manners, filling each miniature plate with little sandwiches, sliced cheese and fruit, and a generous helping of corn chips.

Julianne kept her gaze averted from Sam, who looked achingly handsome in the tuxedo jacket even without a tie or cummerbund. He'd worn a similar tux for their wedding, a dark blue that emphasized the color of his eyes. And on that day his blue eyes had adored her, cherished her, made promises he hadn't kept. With an inward sigh, she focused on Emily's chatter.

"I told Ian when we're twelve we can get married," Emily said. "How old were you, Mommy?"

"I was twenty-one."

"Golly, you were *old!*" Emily exclaimed. Sam laughed as Julianne smiled ruefully.

Sam reached over and covered Julianne's hand with his. "Yes, your mama was quite an old maid, but I decided she was the only old maid I wanted in my life."

"And then you got me," Emily exclaimed. "And now we're a family."

"Yes, now we're a family." Sam's hand gently squeezed Julianne's.

"We're learning about families in school," Emily explained as she poured punch for everyone.

"My teacher says families are important. No matter what happens to us, we always got our family."

Julianne sighed in silent relief as Sam removed his hand from hers. "I'd like to make a toast," he said, raising his glass of punch in the air. "To us . . . to our family." His gaze refocused on Julianne. "No matter what happens, may we always have each other."

Emily laughed in delight as Sam clinked his glass to hers, then did the same with Julianne. Julianne breathed a sigh of relief as the conversation shifted to Emily's favorite cartoons.

She was beginning to wonder if somehow Sam had orchestrated the whole discussion on the importance of family in an attempt to make her feel guilty.

"I think somebody needs a nap," Julianne observed when Emily tried to stifle her third yawn in as many minutes.

"Mr. Bunny is tired," Emily agreed. "And he likes it when I take a nap with him." She turned to Sam. "Daddy, will you tell me a story and sit with me until I'm asleep?"

Sam nodded. "I can't think of anything I'd rather do."

"And while you're doing that, I'll clean up the dishes from the tea party."

"It was a fun tea party, wasn't it?" Emily asked as she crawled up on her bed. "I think it was the bestest one I could ever have."

"It was wonderful," Julianne agreed.

Julianne carried the dishes down to the kitchen and put them in the dishwasher. As she cleaned up the rest of the mess, she tried not to dwell on how nice it had been for the three of them to be together.

She honestly couldn't remember the last time they had all had such a leisurely time. Sam had never had leisure time, or had chosen not to take any. Julianne's heart was filled with aborted attempts at picnics, canceled vacations and social events attended alone.

Finishing the clean-up, she shoved the unpleasant memories out of her head. She needed to focus on the here and now, not dwell on the past or worry about the future. The past was done, and the future was out of her control. She would make no decisions until Sam's present dilemma was solved.

As she walked back into Emily's room, Sam placed a finger to his lips, indicating that the child was sound asleep. He stood and followed Julianne out into the hallway. "She must have been exhausted, she only heard the beginning of my story before falling asleep," he said.

"Tea parties are exhausting."

"Or my story was boring," he added with a grin. The smile faded and he reached out and touched a strand of her hair, his gaze lingering on her warmly. "I remember the first time you wore that dress," he said, his voice husky as his eyes darkened in hue.

"It was a spring charity dance and we were late because on the way we parked in a grocery store parking lot and made out like a couple of hot teenagers."

Julianne's breath caught in her throat as she remembered that night so many years before. "I remember," she said softly.

"And I danced every dance with you and couldn't wait to get you home and finish what we had started in that parking lot." His fingers moved from her hair to her throat, softly caressing and evoking a remembered heat inside her. "Sweet Juli, come dance with me."

He took her hand and led her into their bedroom where he locked the door then punched on the radio and turned the dial. Soft, easy-listening music filled the air. Then, smiling once again, he pulled her into his arms and moved to the rhythm of the music.

Julianne had always loved dancing with Sam. He led with strength, yet moved with a sensuous grace few men could claim. Their bodies were made to dance together. Her long legs followed his effortlessly, her body molding to the contours of his.

She closed her eyes, wanting to lose herself in the music and the man who held her so tight. She didn't want to think about the trouble they were in. She didn't want to think about whether she would remain with him when it was all over. She only wanted to revel in being held by Sam.

His scent surrounded her, soothing in its familiarity, as warming as his body so close to hers. His hands on her back were hot, burning their imprint through the thin silk material of her dress and reminding her of how much she'd loved to make love with Sam. He was a giving lover, never hurried and always lavish with caresses and kisses.

"Juli." His voice was low and soft in her ear and a shiver danced through her as his lips grazed the vulnerable skin just beneath her earlobe.

"Sam." She frowned and thought of a protest, but as his lips covered hers all thoughts of objecting fell away. His mouth was hot, insistent, demanding her response. Tangling her fingers in the hair at the nape of his neck, she opened her mouth to him, wanting the deep, soul kisses she knew he could give.

This was her husband, her spouse, her mate, and it suddenly seemed crazy that he'd been back in the house, back in her life for two days and they hadn't touched each other intimately, hadn't kissed or made love.

Why had she been punishing him? Why had she been punishing herself? They might not be together next week, or next year, but for now she was here with him.

Without missing a beat, Sam danced them over to the bed, not breaking the kiss. Julianne drank in the taste of him, losing herself in the heat and passion of his lips.

"Oh, Juli," he finally said as his mouth left hers. "There were so many nights I thought I'd never see you again, never hold you again."

"Shh," Julianne whispered, not wanting to talk of the lonely, aching nights. "We're together now and that's all that's important."

He cupped her face in his hands, his eyes glazed with the fever of desire. The same fever suffused her body, causing a tingling, sizzling heat to spread from the pit of her stomach outward.

His mouth captured hers again, his tongue dancing with hers as he worked to remove the tuxedo jacket. As the jacket fell to the floor, Julianne's fingers moved to unfasten the buttons of his shirt, wanting to feel the warmth of his chest, the play of his muscles beneath the smooth flesh.

As the shirt fell away, Julianne caressed the expanse of his chest and pressed one palm against the place where his heart beat frantically, mirroring the beat of her own.

"Juli." He whispered her name and she heard the love in his voice. Tears burned in her eyes, and she didn't know if it was because she loved him or because she was so afraid his love just wasn't enough.

Shoving away the doubts, she surrendered all thoughts to the passion he stirred inside her, the aching desire he evoked.

As he unzipped her dress and his warm hands splayed across her back, she moaned. It had been so long, so very long since she'd felt his touch, rejoiced in his caress.

He gently pulled the top of the dress down her shoulders, exposing her lacy bra to his heated gaze. "You're so beautiful," he breathed. "Every night while I was gone you haunted my dreams, tormenting me because I wanted you so much. I've been so afraid...afraid I wouldn't touch you again, love you again." His lips once again sought hers and the last of Julianne's inhibitions fell away beneath the magic he'd always managed to weave around her, inside her.

Together they sank down onto the bed, the mattress welcoming their combined weight like an old friend's warm embrace. Their bodies automatically found the curves and contours of each other, molding together with the familiarity of long-time lovers.

"Oh, Juli...Juli," Sam whispered against her neck as his hands splayed across her back. "I can't tell you how much I've needed you, wanted you in my arms. Thoughts of you were the only things that kept me sane, kept me fighting to stay alive."

"Shh." Julianne placed a finger against his lips. "I'm here with you now."

"Yes," he agreed, and again in the depths of his eyes she saw questions she couldn't answer. She couldn't promise she'd be with him forever. She wasn't even sure she could promise him tomorrow.

Before she had a chance to say anything more, his lips claimed hers once again, evoking response and beckoning desire. She curled her fingers in his hair, loving the tactile sensation of his silken strands against her fingertips.

The doorbell chimed. Sam's arms tightened around her as he ended their kiss. "Ignore it," he urged.

"I can't do that. My car is out front, people know I'm home. You said it was important we maintain normalcy."

Reluctantly he released his hold on her. As she got up, she pulled the gown back up on her shoulders, then moved to the window and peered out.

"Who is it?" he asked.

She stared out the window at the police car in the driveway, then turned and looked at Sam, her heart beating frantically in her chest. "It's reality," she answered.

Chapter Six

"Mrs. Baker?" The police officer on the front porch was baby-faced, with sandy-brown hair and chocolate-brown eyes. "Are you Mrs. Julianne Baker?"

"Yes. What can I do for you, Officer..."

"Richards. Mike Richards. I'd like to ask you a couple of questions, if you don't mind." He frowned, his gaze taking in her silk dress. "Uh, did I catch you at a bad time?"

"Oh, no. I was just trying on some clothes for a charity drive." Julianne ran her hands nervously down the sides of the dress. "Questions about what?"

"Would it be possible for me to come in?"

No. That was her first knee-jerk reaction to his request. What if Sam made a noise? What if Emily woke up and came bounding downstairs talking about her tea party with Mommy and Daddy? But if she said no, would the officer suspect something? Oh, please, don't let her make the wrong decision. Don't let her make a mistake.

"Mrs. Baker?"

She flushed. "Certainly, please come in." She opened the door and led him into the living room, gesturing to the sofa. "Now, what can I do for you, Officer Richards?" she asked as she perched on the edge of the chair facing him.

He pulled a small notepad and a pen from his breast pocket. Flipping open the pad, he smiled as if to ease her anxiety. It didn't work. Anxiety bubbled in her stomach like a caldron of noxious poisons.

"I'm one of the officers assigned to your father-in-law's murder case," he explained. "You are aware of the fact that we're seeking your husband in connection with the crime."

She nodded, her heart beating a frantic tattoo in her chest. "Ha-have you found him?" she asked. Wasn't it a logical question for a wife to ask about a husband who she wasn't supposed to know his whereabouts?

"No." He eyed her curiously. "Am I right in assuming you've heard nothing from him?"

"That's right." She hoped the lie didn't sound like one. How she hated this, all of it. The deceptions, the necessary lies.

"We got a report that somebody saw your husband carrying your daughter out of the house on the night the smoke bomb was set off," he said, his gaze not wavering from hers.

"That's ridiculous," she scoffed. "Who would say such a thing?" Her mind raced. Who might have seen him? Who had watched Sam step out of the smoking house that night? Who had called the police? Friend or enemy? Again anxiety filled her, making it difficult to breathe.

Officer Richards shrugged. "It was an anonymous call. The captain felt we should come out here and follow up on it."

"There's nothing to follow up. I haven't seen or heard from Sam since the night his father was murdered." Anger surged as the officer's gaze turned skeptical. "Perhaps if the police force wasn't so hell-bent on arresting my husband, you would find the real murderer who killed my father-in-law."

There was a moment of heavy silence. "Who did carry your daughter out of the house that night, Mrs. Baker?"

Julianne frowned, unsure what to say. Obviously somebody in the neighborhood saw a man carry out Emily. "It was a passerby who saw the smoke and ran in to save Emily." She raised her chin and eyed the officer boldly. "It was a miracle, and he was a real hero."

"And what was the hero's name?"

Julianne could tell by his tone of voice that he didn't believe her, but she didn't care. She had to protect Sam until he could straighten things out. Still, she tried to stick as close to the truth as possible. "I don't know what his name was. He came out of the house and placed Emily on the ground next to me, then I passed out. When I came to, the fire department had arrived and the man was gone."

"So we have a shy hero," he replied, making notes on his pad.

Again anger reared up inside Julianne at his slightly mocking tone. "I don't know who he was or why he disappeared. Perhaps he's shy, maybe he didn't want to get involved. I'd love to find out who he is so I can thank him for saving my daughter." She sighed and tried to get hold of her emotions. "All I can tell you is that I would have known if it was Sam who carried Emily out of the house that night."

Tears burned her eyes, tears of frustration, tears formed by lies, a result of not knowing what was best, whom to trust, yet knowing she had to trust Sam. "For God's sake, don't you think I want my husband found?"

"Mrs. Baker, don't get upset." Her tears apparently unsettled the officer. "I had to ask, you know, follow up on the phone call we received."

"Whomever called you was mistaken," she answered as she wiped her cheeks with the backs of her hands. "And I'll tell you this, as long as the police are looking for Sam, they are making a mistake. He's not guilty and someone in Baker Enterprises is a murderer. And while you're looking for the real murderer, how about trying to find out who set off a smoke bomb in my house?"

"Yes, ma'am," he said as he stood to leave. "I'll just let you get back to whatever you were doing. We'll be sure to get in touch with you if we discover anything about the smoke bomb incident."

After ushering him out, Julianne leaned heavily against the door, waiting for her heart to stop the erratic beat that had begun the moment she'd first faced him. When would this all end? When would Sam be free and the lies finally finished?

"Juli?" Sam's soft voice came floating down the staircase.

She turned around. "Yes, he's gone."

He came down the stairs and wrapped his arms around her. Gone was any flicker of the previous desire that had sizzled between them. His arms offered only solace. "Oh, Juli, I'm sorry you're in the position to have to lie. I'm sorry I've put you in the middle of this mess."

Julianne moved out of his arms and smiled. "Sam, I'm supposed to be in the mess with you. You're my husband." A whisper of anger raised up inside her. "That's always been half your problem."

"What?"

"That you handle everything alone. You can't or won't depend on anyone else. You isolate yourself from everyone and that's always made me feel like a useless appendage instead of a vital part of your life." She flushed and shoved a strand of her hair away from her face. "I'm sorry. I know this is the last thing you need to hear from me right now."

The blue of his eyes darkened to the color of midnight. "Perhaps this is something we need to talk about right now," he countered.

Julianne was aware of the strain on his features, the lines of mental exhaustion that cut deeply across his forehead. The time wasn't right to discuss their marital problems. He had enough to handle trying to catch a murderer. "Not now, Sam." She reached up and gently traced the lines etched in the skin beside his eyes. "There will be time for us to talk about us later."

"Julianne, you know I love you," he said.

She nodded. "I know," she answered softly, then straightened her shoulders as if mentally putting the conversation behind her. "And now I've got to get changed and get out of here. This morning I made an appointment for a job interview at four this afternoon.''

"Are you sure you want a job?" Sam asked. "Once things get back to normal, you'll be busy with all kinds of social things with Baker Enterprises.''

"Sam, I have to seek my own dream, separate from you and Baker Enterprises.''

Sam's stomach twisted painfully as he recognized the steel resolve in her eyes. It was the same resolve he'd seen the first time he'd suggested they get a housekeeper. She'd told him she didn't want one, had insisted she needed purpose in her life, even if that purpose was simply keeping a nice house for him.

"I've got to go get ready.''

He watched as she walked up the stairs and disappeared down the hallway, then he leaned against the front door, his heart heavy.

Separate dreams. She needed something separate from him. And for the first time in as long as he could remember, when he'd said he loved her, she hadn't returned the sentiment.

He ran a hand down his face, across his jaw, thinking, reassessing. While on the run, it had been thoughts of Julianne and their life together that had kept him sane. But he realized now his memory had been distinctly selective.

He'd remembered the good times, flashes of memories that had made him feel good. Julianne laughing, her eyes warm as cocoa as her joy filled him up. Julianne, rocking an infant Emily to sleep, the maternal smile on her face a mixture of happiness, mystery and a glowing femininity that stole his breath away. Snapshots of happiness frozen in time, etched in his mind, but having little to do with the reality of his marriage just before he'd disappeared.

This time as his memories played inside his head, they were different, far less pleasant. Julianne, eyes swollen with unshed tears as he came home late once again. Julianne, turning her back to him in bed instead of falling into his arms.

He suddenly realized things had been wrong for a very long time, but he hadn't wanted to deal with it, hadn't wanted to face it.

He was an expert at business negotiations, trouble-shooting problems in the company, but he had no clue as to how to fix his marriage. It had been easier to ignore the problems and hope they went away.

But they hadn't gone away and for the first time Sam realized he wasn't just fighting for his life...he was fighting for his wife.

And something else that bothered him. The policeman's report that somebody had anonymously called them. Had it been a neighbor who'd seen him, they would have joined him, tried to help. Besides, a neighbor wouldn't have remained anonymous.

Somebody had hidden in the shadows that night and watched as he'd carried his daughter out of the house and to safety. His blood ran cold. Somewhere, somebody knew he was here.

"Thank you, Mrs. Walker. I'll see you next Monday morning," Julianne said as she stepped out of the door of the Kids First Daycare.

A job. She got into her car and leaned back, for a moment basking in the joy of accomplishment. She had a job. As of Monday morning she would be a teacher's aide. Sure, it was only part-time and just a bit over minimum wage, but the director, Harriet Walker, had liked some of her ideas and had promised Julianne the latitude and support to implement some of them.

It had been a long time since she'd felt the pleasure of a positive stroke. It felt good, like one of Sam's kisses. She flushed as she remembered how close she had come to making love with him that morning. Oh, his kisses had been seductive, his caresses overwhelming in their fire and familiarity. Even now her body ached with unfulfillment, the desire to finish what they had begun.

Although she hadn't welcomed the police officer at her door, she'd welcomed the interruption. She couldn't fall back into the same patterns, swallowing her unhappiness, allowing the power of their lovemaking to make decisions for her.

That's what she had done before he'd disappeared. She'd settled for a lifetime of hurried kisses and midnight caresses; she'd settled for Sam fitting her into his busy schedule. It wasn't enough. It would never be enough.

The euphoria over the new job disappeared beneath the weight of her thoughts. Starting the engine, she took a deep breath, wondering if Sam had made any headway on cracking Joseph's computer program while she'd been gone. She hoped so. She couldn't think, couldn't make a rational decision concerning her marriage as long as Sam's freedom was at risk.

Driving to the baby-sitter's, she tried to focus instead on the beautiful autumn evening. Twilight painted everything a lush gold tone, imbuing the world with a warmth she wished she could swallow to heat the cold spots inside her.

There had been a brief time long ago when they'd first gotten married when Sam had been her twilight. He'd filled her with warmth, but those days had passed long ago and she feared they would never be able to recapture those golden moments of yesterday.

Two weeks before Sam had disappeared, she'd finally confessed her unhappiness to her mother. "Julianne, the honeymoon can't last forever," her mother had observed.

"I don't expect the honeymoon to last forever. I'd just hoped my marriage would last a little longer," Julianne had replied. "I don't know what scares me more, living the rest of my life with Sam or without him."

Julianne thought of those words now. What had kept her in the marriage was fear...she'd never lived alone, wasn't sure she was capable. Sam's disappearance had taught her she could be alone. She knew now she could function as a single parent, could endure lonely nights and empty days. Of course, she had felt those same things being with Sam.

She pulled into the baby-sitter's driveway and rubbed her forehead wearily. There was nothing more exhausting than trying to make life-altering decisions, especially ones that tore at the heart.

It would be so much easier to make the decision to leave Sam if she no longer loved him. But she did love him. She just wasn't sure she could live the life he offered her any longer.

Emily met her at the door, a bundle of energy and giggles that instantly soothed Julianne's troubling thoughts. "Hi, pumpkin, did you have a good time with Susan?"

"Yup. We did finger painting on the kitchen table." Emily ran to the coffee table where a picture was laid out, apparently drying. "It's a fairy dancing with a unicorn," Emily explained as she handed the picture to Julianne. "Susan says it's abstract."

Julianne laughed as Susan appeared in the doorway between the kitchen and the living room. "It's a beautiful picture," Julianne agreed. "Hi, Susan. Thanks for watching her."

"No problem. We always have fun, right, Emily?" Susan smiled.

"Right," Emily readily agreed. "Susan promised next time she watches me she's gonna show me how to make pictures with macaroni and glue."

"Sounds better than macaroni and cheese," Julianne replied.

Emily tilted her head curiously. "Can you make pictures out of macaroni and cheese?"

"Not in this house." Susan laughed. "As it is I've got to get the finger-painting mess cleaned up before Mom gets home."

"Need some help?" Julianne asked, anxious to get home but not wanting to leave Susan with a mess of her daughter's making.

"Nah. It's no big deal."

"Then we'll get out of your hair. Thanks again." Saying their goodbyes, Julianne and Emily left the house and got into the car.

"Did you get the job, Mommy?" Emily asked as she buckled her seat belt.

"As a matter of fact, I did. Isn't that wonderful?" Julianne looked at her daughter enthusiastically. Emily was silent, her forehead wrinkled in a frown as she studied her seat belt with unnatural intensity. "Emily? What's the matter, honey?"

"Nothing." Still the little girl refused to meet her mother's gaze.

A whisper of worry niggling in the pit of her stomach, Julianne pulled the car over to the curb. She turned and faced her daughter. "Emily, tell me what's wrong." She leaned over and lifted her daughter's chin with her index finger. "Mommies can always tell when something is bothering their children."

Emily's frown deepened and she twirled a strand of her hair, a sure sign that something bothered her. "If you go to work, does this mean I won't see you anymore?"

"Oh, no, sweetheart. In fact, you can come with me to my new job," Julianne replied. "You're going to like it. It's a preschool with lots of fun things to do and lots of kids to play with. They even have a pet rabbit there."

"A rabbit? What's his name?"

"Peter, I think," Julianne answered absently. She frowned and stroked a strand of her daughter's shining hair. "Why did you think my working meant we wouldn't see each other anymore?"

Emily shrugged. "I dunno." She twirled her hair faster, then stopped the motion and looked at Julianne. "When Daddy was going to work, we never saw him. He was never home for tea parties or to tuck me in at night." She smiled and released her hold on her hair. "I like it now that Daddy is a ghost daddy 'cause now he spends lots of time with us and we can have fun together."

A bleak wind of despair blew through Julianne. How sad and how very telling of how things had been before Sam had left. As long as Sam remained a fugitive hiding in their attic, Emily had her daddy and Julianne had her husband.

How heartbreaking it was that when Sam cleared his name he'd go back to his work, back to the company, and Emily would lose her daddy once again. Just as Julianne would lose her husband.

Chapter Seven

Sam stretched with arms overhead, then rubbed the back of his neck tiredly. For the past three days he'd been cooped up in the attic working on cracking the code to the mysterious file. After three days of work, he was beginning to realize how futile his efforts were.

Punching off the power button on the laptop, he stood and once again stretched, trying to unkink muscles and relax the stress that tightened his shoulders.

He'd made it a point each day to take a break and have lunch with Julianne and Emily. They'd even had another tea party, but there had been no slow dancing or lovemaking afterward. In fact, each day he felt Julianne slipping further and further away from him, and that scared the hell out of him.

Sighing in frustration, he went downstairs to make himself something to eat. Julianne and Emily had left early that morning, Julianne as excited as a child on the first day of school as she anticipated beginning her new job.

As he stood in front of the refrigerator, the house surrounded him in silence . . . a silence that pressed heavily on him. He'd grown accustomed to hearing the presence of his wife and daughter while he worked, their voices and laughter comforting him. Without their presence, there was no comfort, only a cold, empty silence and he realized if he lost Julianne, that's what his life would be like...cold and empty.

Was this what it was like for Julianne while he was at work? Did the hours of the day stretched empty and endless? Surely not. Julianne was involved in activities, she had women friends to talk with on the phone, things to do to pass the time.

He slammed the refrigerator door, appetite gone beneath the unappetizing flavor of his thoughts. Sinking down at the table, he burrowed his head in his hands, for a moment overwhelmed with hopelessness. He was never going to crack the file. Julianne was going to leave him and Emily would grow up the child of a broken marriage and with a father in prison for murder.

Perhaps the best thing he could do for them both was let them go. Let them build a new life without him. Julianne was a beautiful woman. Eventually she would find another husband, one who could fill her heart with happiness. Emily was young and loving, and would eventually grow to welcome another daddy without question.

But no matter how rationally he considered this option, his heart wouldn't allow him to *seriously* consider it. He loved Julianne like no other man could, and he couldn't imagine his life without her and Emily. He was Julianne's husband and Emily's father, and he didn't want that to change.

What frightened him was that he knew he was no longer in control. The ball was in Julianne's court. Whether they would have a marriage, a life together, was her decision, her choice.

He froze as a knock banged on the door. The knock was firm, authoritative in sound, and it evoked a moment of panic inside him. Was it the police? This time did they have a warrant? Would they burst into the house and find him here, sitting at the table, nursing regrets instead of a cup of coffee?

His insides jumped as the knock resounded again. Soundlessly, he walked from the kitchen into the hallway, then crept up the stairs to Emily's room where the windows overlooked the driveway. He breathed a sigh of relief as he saw the white Lincoln Town car in the drive. Garrison.

For a moment Sam fought an impulse to run downstairs and open the door, admit the man who had been his father's business partner for years and Julianne's main emotional and financial support while he'd been gone.

Perhaps Garrison could offer some sound advice as to what Sam should do; maybe he'd have an idea on how to get into Joseph's secret file.

Despite the impulse, Sam remained at the window, watching as Garrison got back in his car and drove off down the street. Once again the silence of the house grew to oppressive proportions and his thoughts once again turned to his wife.

It was time he and his wife had a talk about where their marriage was going. He needed to know how she felt, what she wanted. She was sending him too many mixed signals. On the one hand, he felt her distance, knew she was emotionally and physically withdrawing from him. Yet on the other hand, he felt her gaze lingering on him often, her eyes mirroring what he perceived as love.

If she did love him and wanted to live a life with him, then he would do everything in his power to make her happy. He knew there had been mistakes made in the past and he would do what he could to rectify those errors.

One thing was certain, he needed to know that if he fought to clear his name and get his life back, that Julianne intended to be a part of that life.

He waited until late that evening, after Emily had gone to bed. They had shared a pleasant dinner together. Julianne loved her new job and spent the meal telling Sam each and every detail of her day. He listened absently, focusing instead on the brightness of her eyes, the beauty of her smile. It had been a very long time since he'd seen her so happy. A tinge of guilt gnawed at him as he remembered how many times she'd tried to talk to him about needing something of her own and his own countering that she had enough to do in being wife of the vice-president of Baker Enterprises.

He'd dismissed her needs, her obvious desires, because he'd been blinded to everything but the family business. He hadn't wanted to think she needed anything but him. He'd been a selfish, foolish man.

It was with this in mind that he went searching for Julianne. He found her in the bedroom. He entered the room just as she stepped out of the adjoining bathroom wrapped only in a towel. "Oh, sorry," he exclaimed, finding it strange to be embarrassed at catching her nearly undressed. "I—I wondered if we could talk."

"Could you give me just a few minutes to get changed?" she asked, her cheeks pinkened with a blush. She looked pointedly at the door.

"Sure. I'll just wait out in the hall." He stepped outside and closed the door behind him, suddenly aware of how mixed up and dysfunctional their marriage had become.

She was his wife, yet she hadn't wanted to dress in front of him. Somehow they had lost the intimacy that formed a good marriage.

He closed his eyes, remembering how it had been when they first got married. They'd often showered together, drying each other then falling onto the bed to make love.

He imagined himself slowly removing her towel, his hands caressing the silky softness of her skin, his mouth kissing the spot behind her ear that always made her moan. Her skin would be damp, flushed from the heat of her bath and would smell of the floral bath oil she often used.

He drew in a deep breath to steady the desire that instantly flared at his thoughts. He wanted it back... the intimacy, the lovemaking, his marriage. He wanted to taste the skin of her flat stomach, feel her arms entwined around his neck as her body pressed against his with need.

He jumped and turned as the door creaked open. "Okay," she said, this time dressed in a blue silk nightgown and matching filmy robe. Her hair was caught up in a ponytail, damp tendrils clinging to her neck and forehead. She sat on the edge of the bed and looked at him expectantly. "What did you want to talk about?" she asked.

He sat down next to her, able to smell the sweet scent of her bubble bath mingling with the minty odor of soap. His body responded to the scent of her and the lingering thoughts of their lovemaking in the past.

"Us." He cleared his throat, reaching for control. He knew she wouldn't welcome any kind of a sexual advance from him, and in truth, although he would love to physically possess her, that wasn't what he needed most from her at the moment. "We need to talk about us."

"Sam." Her brow wrinkled and she gave him a look filled with pain. "I don't think now is the time to talk about us. We have a lot of hurdles to get over before we can begin to even *think* about us and any kind of a future we might have together."

"Julianne, I need to talk about it now." He raked a hand through his hair, his gaze lingering on her, trying to read what was in her mind, in her heart. "During dinner tonight I saw your eyes sparkling as you told me about your day at work, and I realized it had been a long time since I'd seen your eyes sparkle with such enthusiasm, such life."

He reached out and took her hand in his. Enclosing it, he felt a flare of hope as she responded by squeezing his. "I've been wrong in encouraging you to be a stay-at-home wife, expecting you to find satisfaction in hosting business dinners and charity functions. I was wrong in not supporting and encouraging you to find something fulfilling, something that made you happy."

She nodded, then sighed. "But, Sam, your support of my working or lack of support is not the real issue."

"Then tell me what is the issue. Tell me what is wrong so I can fix it." He squeezed her hand. "Julianne, I'm working as hard as I can to crack that file and clear my name. But it doesn't mean anything if when I finally succeed you aren't there beside me. If I can't count on you being with me when this whole mess is worked out, then what's the point? If I've lost you, then I might as well just turn myself in to the police now and let them throw me into prison for the rest of my life."

She snatched her hand from his, her eyes shooting fires of anger. "That's not fair, Sam." She got up off the bed, her movements jerky as she walked several paces away. She turned back and glared at him. "How dare you put the pressure on me? If you're going to fight to clear your name, you do it for yourself. This isn't a game show where you win the contest and get to keep your wife as a prize."

"Juli." Sam rose and walked to where she stood, trembling with the emotion of her outburst. "You're right, that wasn't fair of me. I just need to know that when this is all over, we still have a marriage. I want a life with you, Julianne, and I need to know you want the same thing."

Her anger escaped her with a heavy sigh and her eyes held a sadness that twisted his insides. "Sam, I wish I could tell you that when this is all over, no matter what the outcome, our marriage will be intact, but I can't make any promises." She smiled, a bittersweet expression. Tilting her head, she looked at him, again her eyes holding a profound sadness. "Does that sound familiar?" she asked.

He shook his head and gazed at her curiously. "Does what sound familiar?"

"I can't make any promises. You used to say that to me each time I asked you if you'd be home for supper, or if you could make it to a particular event. You'd always say, 'I don't know, Juli. I can't make any promises.'"

He took a step closer to her. "Is... is there somebody else?"

She looked at him incredulously. "You think I might have a lover?" She laughed, a bitter sound that jarred his insides. "Oh, that's rich. If I had a lover, we probably wouldn't be having this conversation. I'd be happy living two lives and wouldn't be considering a divorce." She shook her head. "No, Sam, there isn't anyone else. There never has been anyone but you."

"Are you telling me you don't love me anymore?" he asked softly.

"No." She smiled and placed a hand on his cheek, her fingers cool and slightly trembling. "I'll always love you, Sam." Her hand dropped back to her side. "I just don't know if I'm in love with you anymore." She bit her bottom lip, her eyes dark with confusion. "Sam, I can't make any promises where our future together is concerned. I just can't.''

He nodded, a black despair washing over him. Too late. The months of unhappiness prior to his disappearance combined with the months he'd been gone had combined to create a situation he didn't know how to handle.

It wasn't until he was back up in the attic, staring blankly at the computer screen that he realized it might not be too late. He'd seen the confusion that darkened her eyes, heard the uncertainty in her voice when she'd said she wasn't sure if she was in love with him any longer. She wasn't sure. That implied hope.

He'd done it once. Surely he could do it once again. Hopefully he could make his wife fall in love with him again. But first he had to clear his name and make certain he actually had a future to share with her.

"I'm just afraid it's too late." Julianne couldn't quite meet Colleen Baker's eyes. Sam's youngest sister had always hero-worshiped her brother, and this was one of the most difficult conversations Julianne knew she would ever have.

Colleen had called several days earlier, wanting to meet Julianne for lunch. With Julianne's new work schedule and Colleen's busy days as a social worker, they finally arranged to meet Thursday evening for dinner at a restaurant located halfway between their two homes.

"Oh, Julianne, it just breaks my heart to hear you say that," Colleen said as she stabbed her fork into a cucumber from her salad. "You and Sam belong together. I can't imagine either one of you without the other."

"I was without my 'other' for four months," Julianne reminded Colleen.

"Yes, but through no fault of his own," Colleen said pointedly.

"I know that." Julianne eyed her sister-in-law curiously. "My feelings for Sam really don't have anything to do with the four months he was gone. I was feeling this same way before he disappeared. The only thing his disappearance did was make me realize I can live without him."

"But do you really want to?" Colleen asked.

"I don't know," Julianne answered in frustration. She placed a chunk of fresh tomato into her mouth then chewed thoughtfully. Even though Sam had cautioned her about telling anyone that he was in the house, she had told Colleen. The tears of relief that had shone in Colleen's eyes had justified Julianne's decision to tell. "If Sam finally manages to straighten out his legal mess, I just don't know if I can go back to the life we had together. I'm afraid of waking up one morning to discover I'm old and my life is behind me and I've sacrificed too much time with the wrong man."

"But how do you know he's the wrong man?" Colleen leaned across the table. "He's been the right man for a long time. Can you just let it all go? Eight years of marriage just thrown away?"

Julianne flushed. "You don't understand. You can't understand. You're a newlywed, still in the honeymoon phase of your marriage."

Colleen reached over and took Julianne's hand. "But I understand unhappiness, and it breaks my heart to see you so unhappy." She released Julianne's hand and instead fumbled with her napkin. "And I also know it will break Sam's heart if you leave him."

"That's not fair," Julianne protested.

Colleen grinned. "Sam is my brother. I don't have to play fair." Her smile faded. "Seriously, Julianne. What has made you unhappy? What is so bad about your marriage that makes you consider throwing it all away?"

Julianne twirled her fork in her salad, trying to gather her thoughts. When had it started going wrong? "I always knew how important the family business was to Sam and his father. Sam's drive and ambition was part of what attracted me to him in the first place." She frowned in frustration. "But the last couple of years I've begun to feel like I'm Sam's mistress and his work is his wife."

"Have you told him how you feel?"

"About a million times. A couple of months before he disappeared I told him. He promised to change things, but nothing changed. If anything he spent more time at work. I don't want to be a whiner or a nag, but I'm tired of empty promises and an empty marriage." She put down her fork and pushed the remainder of her salad aside. "What scares me most of all is that sometimes I think Sam works so many hours because subconsciously he doesn't want to be at home with me." Tears burned at her eyes with the confession of her fear.

"Oh, Julianne." Again Colleen's hand reached for hers, squeezing her fingers in sympathy. Colleen sighed, her blue eyes, so like Sam's, troubled. She released Julianne's hand and leaned back in her chair, her gaze thoughtful. "Has Sam ever talked to you about our childhood?"

Julianne shrugged. "Bits and pieces, although nothing real specific. Why?"

"Just curious." She smiled ruefully. "It's funny, most people think we must have had an idyllic childhood. Although our mother died when we were all young, our father was wealthy, the respected owner of a large corporation. We went to the best schools, wore the latest fashions, traveled extensively. But the children of Camelot weren't always happy." She hesitated a moment, then continued. "I have a feeling when Sam is spending so many hours at work it isn't that he's running away from you. It's what he thinks he's running toward, not away from."

Julianne frowned. "I'm not sure I understand."

Colleen smiled and waved her hands in a dismissive gesture. "Forget it. I have no right trying to analyze my big brother. Besides, if you really want to know about Sam's childhood and his possible motivations for being a workaholic, you need to ask Sam." Colleen took a sip of her water. "Now, let's talk of something more pleasant. How's the new job?"

"I love it," Julianne answered without hesitation. "I never realized how much joy there'd be in getting up and getting dressed in the mornings to do work that helps others." She smiled ruefully at Colleen's grin. "I know, I know. You're thinking why is it okay for me and not okay for Sam, but I work eight hours five days a week and still have a family life. Sam works twelve hours seven days a week and doesn't have a family life."

"Point taken," Colleen replied.

"So tell me about that handsome husband of yours. Marriage definitely agrees with you. You're positively glowing." A wistful stir of envy bubbled inside Julianne as she recognized the utter happiness that shone on Colleen's face.

"Gideon is wonderful. He's all that I dreamed of and more."

"I can't thank you and Gideon enough for what you did for Sam. He told me he came to see you, about Gideon thinking he was a burglar and wrestling him to the ground. Gideon could have turned him in to the police, made quite a name for himself in nabbing the elusive fugitive.''

Colleen nodded. ''Yes, he could have. But he trusted me, and I trust Sam.'' She reached for Julianne's hand across the table. ''And I'm sorry I couldn't tell you about seeing Sam. He made me promise not to. It was the most difficult promise I've ever had to keep and I hope you aren't angry with me.''

''Oh, Colleen, I'm too confused about this whole mess to be angry about anything.''

''Sam hasn't had any luck in breaking into the computer program?'' Colleen asked, lowering her voice so their conversation wouldn't be overheard by the other diners in the restaurant.

''No. It seems an impossible task without the other two charms. But he's spending hours at the computer, systematically trying combinations of numbers and letters.''

Colleen shook her head. ''There's got to be another way. It could take him years to finally hit upon the right combination.''

''If only somebody else hadn't stolen Carolyn's and Bonnie's charms,'' Julianne said. ''Sam is certain it was somebody from the corporation who stole them, somebody who wants into that computer program as badly as he does.''

''Does he have any idea who it might be?''

''No, although it would have to be someone in a position of power.''

Colleen frowned. "That could be a dozen or more people."

Julianne rubbed her forehead wearily. "I know. If we knew who we could trust we'd get someone within the company to help us, but..." She spread her hands out in a gesture of helplessness. "Sam has never been very good at trusting others to do what he can do."

"Just make sure the two of you remember that Gideon and I will do anything we can to help."

"I know." Julianne smiled appreciatively, knowing Colleen was as good as her word.

"And thank you for telling me he's safe. I've been so worried since the night he left my house."

Julianne nodded. "It's not over yet. The night of the smoke bomb somebody saw Sam carry Emily out of the house and they went to the police. An officer came to the house the other day asking questions. I'm afraid one of these days they'll show up with a search warrant and Sam will be arrested."

"He's got to get into that file," Colleen exclaimed. "It's the only thing that will vindicate Sam." Colleen looked at Julianne, her expression somber. "And if Sam doesn't manage to clear his name, you won't have to worry about making a decision about a separation from him. He'll go to prison for the rest of his life."

As Julianne drove home, Colleen's words replayed in her head. If her marriage didn't work she wanted it to be her decision to let it go. She didn't want a choice made by default because he was imprisoned for a crime he didn't commit.

It took her only a few minutes to drive by Susan's and pick up Emily, then the two of them drove the short distance home. Julianne's stomach clenched into a tight knot as she recognized Barry's car in the driveway.

He got out of his car as they pulled in. "I was just about to give up and go home," he said as they got out of the car and approached him.

"Just getting off work?" Julianne asked.

He nodded. "But I promised Miranda no matter how late I got off that I'd stop by and invite you and Emily to dinner on Saturday. How's my favorite little brat?" he asked, swinging Emily up on his hip.

"I'm not a brat," Emily protested as she playfully pulled on his nose.

Julianne's mind raced as Barry walked with them to the front door. She knew Barry would think it odd if she didn't invite him in. She just hoped Sam was hidden away in his attic retreat. "Come on in, Barry," she said as she opened the door, hoping her voice wasn't so loud Barry would think her strange and hoping Sam heard her and did a disappearing act.

Barry followed her into the kitchen, Emily riding his hip like a baby koala bear. "Where have you been? It's not like you to be out in the evenings?" he asked.

"I had dinner with Colleen," Julianne explained. "I'm working now, so we decided to meet for a fast supper and catch up on things."

"So, you got a job." Barry sat down at the table, Emily on his lap.

Julianne quickly filled him in on her new position. "Want me to make some coffee?" she asked.

"No, it's late. I've got to get home. So, what do you say about Saturday? You two want to come over for the day?"

"Mommy, what about our tea parties with Daddy?" Emily asked.

"Honey, why don't you run on upstairs and get ready for bed? It's getting late." Julianne waited until Emily had left the room, then she faced Barry, whose features wore the expression of suspicious curiosity.

"Tea parties with Daddy?"

Julianne nodded. "It's a way to keep her close to Sam. We have tea parties and Sam is the official guest of honor."

Barry frowned. "Do you really think it's wise to indulge Emily in her fantasies?"

Julianne sighed. "Barry, I really don't know what's wise and what isn't anymore. Look, with my new job, things have been kind of frantic around here. I was looking forward to having Saturday to catch up on things around here. Can I have a rain-check?"

"Sure," he agreed, although Julianne could still see a whisper of suspicion in his eyes. She breathed a sigh of relief as he stood and headed for the front door. She walked with him, her heart thudding as he paused and turned back to her. "You'd tell me if Sam was here, wouldn't you?" he asked.

"Of course," she answered, the words feeling wooden as they fell from her lips.

His gaze seemed to see right through her, right to the lies. "You know I'm your friend, Julianne. I'm Sam's friend, and he's in a whole lot of trouble. He's accustomed to being a solitary kind of man, but this is bigger than he can handle alone. When you're ready for help you know where to find me."

Julianne watched him go, sick at heart, knowing that time was running out.

Chapter Eight

"I'm sure he didn't believe me," Julianne told Sam later that night. She sat next to him on a blanket spread on the floor of his attic hideaway.

He'd made himself a fairly comfortable niche by moving some of the boxes and crates to give himself more room, then spreading a quilt and blanket down for a bed.

"Are you sure?" Sam's features were barely visible in the moonlight seeping in the attic vents. They didn't dare turn on any lights, afraid the illumination would be seen by somebody outside the otherwise darkened house.

"Positive. I could tell just by the way he looked. He suspects you're here."

He covered his face with his hands, his shoulders slumping forward in defeat. Julianne's heart ached for him. Sam had always been so dynamic, so strong and in control. She wasn't accustomed to seeing him so vulnerable, so hopeless. "Sam, maybe we should just tell Barry the truth, that you're here and trying to break into the computer file. He's your friend. Maybe he can help."

Sam removed his hands from his face. "And maybe he's the one who made the anonymous call to the police."

Julianne sucked in a breath. "Surely you don't believe that. Not Barry?"

He shrugged. "I don't know what to believe, who to trust. All I know is somebody my father trusted killed him, and, as head of security, my father would have trusted Barry. Barry also has lots of friends on the police force. It would be easy for him to set me up."

"But, Sam, he's been our friend for a long time," Julianne protested softly, finding this kind of betrayal difficult to believe.

He nodded, the lines of his face deep with weariness. "Juli, the corporation was laundering large amounts of money, and money often makes friendships worthless."

Julianne leaned against his side, wishing she could remove the stress that darkened his eyes and puckered the skin across his forehead. He put his arm around her, pulling her more comfortably against him. His white T-shirt smelled of fresh-scented detergent and bleach and the subtle spicy scent of his cologne. "Time is running out, Juli, and I'm no closer to cracking that file than I was a week ago...two weeks ago."

She shivered, scared because she didn't know who they could trust, and afraid they wouldn't clear Sam's name without help. "What are you going to do?" she asked softly.

"I don't know." He wiped a hand across his jaw, then rubbed the point of his forehead directly between his eyes.

"Headache?" she asked.

He let his hand fall back to his side and smiled at her. "I've had a headache for the last four months. If it ever finally goes away I'll feel like something's missing." His smile slowly faded and he heaved a deep sigh. "Maybe I should just give up, turn myself in and face the consequences."

"No, Sam. That's not a viable option if you're sure they'll put you in prison and the real killer will remain free."

He raised a dark eyebrow and looked down at her in wry amusement. "Ah, Juli, I wasn't sure you cared." Despite his light tone, she heard the serious undertone he attempted to hide.

"Sam." She laid a hand on his chest, turning slightly so she could see into his eyes. "You know better than that. No matter what happens between the two of us, I'd never want to see you in jail for a

crime you didn't commit." She took his hand in
hers and for the first time noticed he wasn't wearing his wedding ring. An unexpected twang of pain
tweaked her heart. "Why aren't you wearing your
ring?" she asked, surprised by how the sight of his
naked finger bothered her.

"It was stolen from me while I was in Casey's
Corners." His voice was soft, but filled with emotional trauma.

"Oh, Sam." Once again she leaned into his side,
wondering what horrors he'd endured while he'd
been on the run and unsure if she wanted to know.

"I fell asleep in an alley behind a café. I was
awakened with a knife to my throat. The man was
apparently a vagrant, but there was a madness in
his eyes that made me instantly realize he'd use the
knife if I gave him reason. He took my wallet and
my ring, then disappeared back into the night.
Needless to say, I didn't go back to sleep."

"A man was found dead in Casey's Corners. He
had your identification on him."

"How do you know that?"

"Bonnie told me a month or so after the fact.
She went in to identify the body. She was afraid it
was you." Julianne shivered, still able to remember the fear that had coursed through her when
Sam's sister had relayed that particular information. She had also heard a strength in Bonnie's
voice she'd never heard before.

He shook his head. "Poor Bonnie. I'm sure she would have rather been in Europe, sipping champagne and dancing until dawn."

"Not anymore," Julianne explained. "When Bonnie went out to Casey's Corners and met Russ, she changed."

"Changed how?" he asked.

"She changed from a flighty party brat to a warm, giving woman. It sounds so trite, but she seemed to find herself and has learned to like who she is. I suspect it has a lot to do with Russ and Russ's son, Daniel. From what I've heard, Russ is a wonderful man and Bonnie has been on cloud nine since their wedding. She told me she never dreamed she'd ever be a mother, and couldn't believe how much she loved mothering Daniel."

"I'm just glad she's happy."

They fell silent. Julianne closed her eyes, allowing Sam's scent to wash over her, his body heat to warm her. If only they could remain here forever, safe from the world in their attic cocoon.

She opened her eyes, knowing it was an unrealistic wish. In her heart she knew even if they could remain here forever, she would never be enough to make Sam happy.

Sam needed the outside world, thrived on the daily stress of high finance and pressure deals. And in truth, she didn't want a life of Sam exclusively devoted to her. She just wanted a life of balance, and Sam seemed incapable of that. She suddenly remembered her conversation with Colleen. "Sam, tell me about your childhood."

She felt his surprise at the question in the way his body tensed then relaxed once again. "My childhood? What do you want to know?" She heard the perplexity in his voice.

"I don't know . . . was it a happy childhood?"

"As good as most, better than some. Why?"

"I don't know. Just curious." Julianne wondered what Colleen had been talking about. "You rarely ever talked about it."

He shrugged. "Not much to say about it. I grew up and that's that. Besides, I've always been the type to look ahead, not back."

Once again Julianne fell silent and Sam followed suit. She didn't know what Colleen had been hinting at, but obviously Sam and Colleen had very different perspectives on their childhoods. Not so unusual considering the fact that Sam was twelve years older than Colleen.

As his hand stroked through her hair, she felt herself relaxing fully against him, enjoying the softness of his caresses. She fought the impulse to turn toward him, place her lips on his and drink in his essence, give herself over to the pleasurable act of making love with him.

She didn't want to confuse him, didn't want to confuse herself, and yet she longed for him to take her. It had been so long, and her body ached to be a part of his. The thought of never again knowing the sheer joy of making love with him filled her with a deep, abiding sadness.

Despite their brief times together in their everyday life, in spite of her growing unhappiness throughout the past couple of years, he'd always made her forget everything by taking her in his arms. Making love had always been the one thing they did tremendously well together.

She closed her eyes once again, allowing sweet memories to wash over her. Sam's mouth on hers, his hands softly touching, caressing her body with flames. Her heart responded to the heat of her thoughts, beating the rapid, uneven rhythm of desire.

Just one last time, she told herself. Why not make love with him one last time? Why deprive herself of the pleasure of being held in his arms, possessed by his fire? At least for this moment they were married, husband and wife.

She turned so she faced him and realized his thoughts must have followed the way of hers, for his eyes were darkened by need and beneath her hand on his chest she could feel the thundering of his heartbeat.

He didn't give her a chance to voice what she wanted; rather, he seemed to sense her need and responded by placing his lips on hers. His mouth plied hers softly, gently, then deepened to taste of fire and need.

With a deft movement, he changed positions, stretching out and pulling her to lie on top of him. During the shifting, their lips never parted.

Julianne wanted to capture each sensation, every sensory detail in her mind. She wanted to always remember the sweet taste of his mouth, the heat of his hands that burned through the back of her thin silk blouse.

"Juli," he breathed as their kiss finally ended. His voice was husky, deeper than usual, and she heard the unspoken question in his tone.

"Shh." She pressed her fingertip to his lips, not wanting to speak, wanting only to follow through on her desire without thought, without explanation, without regrets.

When his mouth covered hers again, gone was any lingering hesitation. This time he tasted of urgency and hunger. She melted against him, her body conforming with intimacy and sweet familiarity into the contours of his.

Julianne had always loved Sam's kisses and this time was no different. For several minutes she was satisfied with the simple pleasure of his mouth on hers. However, it didn't take long before she wanted more.

Again Sam understood her need. With one swift movement he pulled his T-shirt over his head, then with his gaze holding hers, he unfastened the buttons of her blouse and removed it from her. As he unsnapped her bra and it fell away, Julianne felt no shyness, no embarrassment, as his gaze lingered on her bareness.

As his hands cupped her breasts, Julianne moaned her pleasure and returned the caress, stroking the strong muscles of his chest, the flat planes of his abdomen. She was vaguely aware of their ragged breaths filling the confines of the attic, aware that she was quickly losing all control beneath the onslaught of his caresses.

Sam knew just where to touch, where to kiss to ignite scorching flames inside her. Partly instinct, mostly familiarity, he'd always managed to take Julianne to the soaring heights of passion. And this time was no different.

Within a few minutes they were both naked and Julianne felt tears pressing heavily at her eyes as Sam weaved his sensual magic, taking her higher and higher. As he possessed her completely, she clung to him. There were no regrets of the past, no concerns for the future. She gave herself totally to the here and now of being in Sam's arms, joined to him body and soul.

Later, she remained in his arms, their breaths slowing, their heartbeats resuming a more normal rhythm. The tears she had fought to hold back flowed freely. Her crying was a common thing. Nearly every time they made love, tears flowed from Julianne.

Sam had teased her on their wedding night, proclaiming that instead of a blushing bride, he'd managed to get a crying bride. Her tears weren't ones of sadness, but rather tears of overwhelming emotion pulled forth from the intensity of sharing so intimately with Sam.

He took his finger and gently wiped her cheeks. "Was it that bad?" he asked teasingly.

It was an old joke and Julianne smiled through her tears. "No. It was that good," she replied. Sam's resulting chuckle swept through her like a welcome cool breeze on a stifling summer day.

She closed her eyes as a renewed arrow of emotion pierced through her and she recognized her tears this time were different. These tears were new, distinct because they grew from a profound sadness that felt like lead in the bottom of her heart. This time she knew she was crying because she'd just made love with her husband for the very last time.

Sam awoke feeling better than he had since his father's murder. Although he was once again alone on the blanket in the attic, Julianne's scent still lingered around him, reminding him of the sweet wonder of their lovemaking. For the first time since his disappearance, hope was back in his heart.

Surely if Julianne really intended to leave him, she wouldn't have made love with him so passionately. She couldn't have faked the desire he saw shining from her eyes. She couldn't pretend it hadn't been love they had expressed by physical means. In their lovemaking, Sam wanted to believe he felt a renewed commitment from her.

Again he felt the shifting sands of time running out, the need to vindicate himself and get his life back to normal. What good was it if Julianne gave him another chance and he ended up in prison for the rest of his life?

He looked at his wristwatch, realizing he'd slept longer and harder than usual. It was after eight, and he was sure Julianne and Emily had already left for the preschool. He'd take a quick shower, then hit the computer. Maybe today would be the day he would crack the file that could free him from his attic hideaway.

Almost nine hours later, the hope he'd had in beginning the day had dwindled to nothing. He set the table, knowing Julianne would appreciate the gesture when she got home. He'd also taken out steaks to broil and had potatoes baking in the oven and a salad chilling in the refrigerator. At least for today he couldn't offer her a future, but he could offer her dinner.

He smiled humorlessly at this thought and sat down at the table. He'd only set two places, afraid that if somebody came in with Julianne after work they would notice a place setting for three.

Barry had almost caught him the night before when he'd walked in with Julianne. Thank goodness Julianne's voice had been loud when she'd entered the house, giving Sam enough time to flee up the stairs.

Barry. Could he be the man behind the murder? The thought made Sam's heart ache with betrayal. Sam had always considered Barry a good friend, but he knew Barry was ambitious, and ambition had ruined many a good man. Now Barry's wife was pregnant, a pregnancy he suspected wasn't a planned one. Had Barry panicked, decided to throw his hand in with criminals for a bonus cash award? Had the thought of a family made Barry decide to pursue money over all else?

He tensed as the front door opened, then relaxed as he heard Julianne's voice. "Sam?" she called, letting him know she and Emily were alone.

"In here." He stood and smiled as Emily launched herself toward him.

"Hi, Daddy. I had a good day," she exclaimed.

"That's terrific. I like it when my girls have good days," he replied, nuzzling her sweet cheek with his nose.

She giggled and twisted out of his arms, a whirlwind of energy. "I made you a picture," she said as she pulled a crayon drawing out of her backpack. "That's me and Mommy and you and Uncle Garri and Aunt Letta, and we're all riding on a dragonfly's back."

"And it's a beautiful dragonfly," Sam observed. He looked at Julianne. She leaned against the cabinet, looking tired but lovely. "Hard day?" he asked.

She shook her head. "Not really. I'm just tired." She gestured toward the table. "Thanks for getting dinner started."

"No problem. I didn't have anything better to do." Despite his effort to the contrary, he heard the hopeless depression in his voice.

"No progress on the file?"

"None worthwhile."

"Emily, run upstairs and put your backpack away, then wash your hands for dinner," Julianne said. As the little girl disappeared from the kitchen, Julianne sank down at the table across from Sam. "I've been thinking, Sam."

He forced a small smile. "Uh-oh."

A flash of responding humor lightened her eyes for a single moment, then she sobered and her eyes darkened. "There's got to be another way to clear your name. It's obvious that cracking that file is going to take months...months I'm afraid we don't have."

He nodded and released a sigh of resignation. "Yeah, I'm beginning to think the same thing. But I don't know what else to do. I don't know who to trust, so I'm afraid to ask anyone to help me. But without help I may not be able to clear my name."

She leaned toward him, her brow wrinkled in thought. "You've got the two charms, yours and Colleen's, right?"

He fought the impulse to take his finger and rub away the worry lines on her forehead. He'd do anything to relieve her of this burden. But he was out of ideas, didn't know how to solve the problems that weighed so heavily on them both. "Yes, but they don't do me a damn bit of good. I need Carolyn's and Bonnie's charms in order to have the complete password to get into the computer program."

"And we don't know who has those charms, but you're fairly sure it's somebody within the corporation."

He nodded agreement. "Nothing else makes sense."

"Sam, why couldn't I pretend I received your and Colleen's charms through the mail and I don't know why you mailed them to me? Why couldn't I go to the Baker Enterprises offices and let people know I have those two charms?"

"Absolutely not." Sam's stomach rolled at the thought of his wife using herself as bait. He stood and turned on the broiler, then shoved the steaks into the oven.

"But don't you agree that might flush out whoever is responsible for all of this mess?" she asked. "They need your charms as badly as you need the ones they have. They'll want to destroy that file before anyone can get to it and use it against them."

"Julianne, forget it. It's a crazy idea. It's too dangerous. I'd never allow you to do such a thing."

Her cheeks flushed red. "But I'm supposed to lie to all our friends and pretend my daughter has a daddy-fantasy problem and live a lie until you manage to stumble across the right combination of numbers and letters?" She drew in a deep, unsteady breath. "For God's sake, Sam. Let me help. At least let me try it and see what happens. Who knows when the police are going to show up at our door with a warrant? Then we'll be out of time, and everything will be out of our control."

Sam sank down in the chair opposite her, torn between warring emotions. On one hand, he knew she was right. They didn't have the luxury of time that it would take for him to crack the file by trial and error. But, dread coursed through him as he considered sending her on a fishing expedition using herself as bait. The person or persons they sought had killed once. There was nothing to assure they wouldn't kill again.

"Juli, I appreciate the offer, but it's just too dangerous. If you connect with the right person they might take you into the parking lot and kill you for those charms."

"Then I won't go in alone," she countered.

He smiled wryly. "I can't exactly be your escort."

She frowned thoughtfully, then snapped her fingers and smiled. "I'll take Colleen with me. We'll get Gideon to wire us." She reached across the table and grabbed his hand. "Sam, I'll do whatever it takes to get this settled and over with. We've got to get on with our lives.''

Sam nodded. Yes, he wanted that more than anything. He wanted to be able to take his daughter to the zoo, or play a game of tag with her in the front yard. He wanted to be able to answer his phone or open his door. More than anything, he wanted to be able to sleep with his wife in his own bed. He wanted to do all those things without the fear that had twisted his insides for the past four months.

He looked at his wife, taking a moment to drink in her features. The dark brown eyes that spoke eloquently of her emotions. The smooth jawline and slightly stubborn thrust of her chin. The mouth that seemed to beg to be kissed. How he loved her. The thought of anything happening to her was enough to make him feel ill, and yet he knew she was at a breaking point.

''Okay,'' he agreed wearily. ''Let's get Colleen and Gideon over here and talk about the possibilities. I'm not saying I agree to this crazy scheme,'' he cautioned, then added, ''but I'm willing to at least discuss it.''

As Julianne went to the phone and dialed Colleen's number, Sam leaned his head down on the tabletop, praying they weren't making an enormous mistake.

Chapter Nine

Monday morning Julianne awakened, nerves tingling, knowing today was the day she might face a murderer. She'd put Emily on a plane the night before. Carolyn had called several hours later to report the little girl had arrived safe and sound and would be a welcomed visitor for the next week or so.

Julianne had called her boss at the preschool yesterday and asked for the day off. She hadn't offered any explanation, just that she had some personal business to take care of.

She rolled over onto her side and looked at the clock. Just after six. Colleen and Gideon would arrive within an hour and they'd finalize their game plan. She frowned, aware that in this particular game the stakes were high . . . life and death.

However, the rewards were enormous. Hopefully, by using herself and the charms as bait, she could give Sam back his life. It would be her final gift to him.

She shoved away this thought, finding it too distracting, too painful to consider. She didn't want anything in her mind except the trip to Baker Enterprises. She needed to remain clearheaded and unemotional, stay focused on her goal. She couldn't think about the fact that when this was over and Sam's name was cleared, she intended to leave him.

Closing her eyes, she tried to steady the nerves that caused her stomach to jump and twitch. She only hoped this worked and she managed to flush out the guilty party. She needed this to be over, needed to begin fresh, start a new life . . . seek the kind of happiness she couldn't seem to find here with Sam.

"Juli?"

She sat up as the person in her thoughts poked his head into the bedroom. "It's okay. I'm awake," she replied.

He walked into the room and sat down on the end of the bed. "Changed your mind about going to Baker Enterprises this morning?"

"No, and nothing is going to change my mind." She pushed a strand of her hair away from her face.

"We have to give it a try, Sam. We're out of choices and we're running out of time."

Her cheeks warmed beneath the weight of his gaze. Was he remembering their lovemaking? She'd tried not to dwell on it, not wanting to remember how good it had felt to be held in his arms, loved so tenderly, so completely.

Would he hate her when she left? Sam was an all or nothing kind of man. She couldn't imagine remaining friends with him when their marriage broke apart, but knew they would be civil for Emily's sake. Civil. It sounded so cold, so impersonal.

"You scared?" he asked.

She nodded. Yes, she was scared...scared of what they were about to do, frightened of leaving him, afraid not to.

"Good," he replied. "It's good if you're scared. That will make you cautious." His gaze lingered on her face. "I still wish there was some other way."

"Me, too," she said, aware she was thinking of something far different from her trip to the Baker Enterprises. "I'd better get showered and dressed. Colleen and Gideon will be here soon."

He nodded and stood. "I'll make the coffee."

Moments later as Julianne stood beneath the shower, she once again thought of her marriage and the man who was her husband. She knew she'd never love a man again in the same way she loved

Sam. She'd never again be quite so naive or filled with such hope.

But even if she never fell in love again, even if she lived the rest of her life alone, it couldn't be as lonely as she'd been during her married life to Sam.

Waiting for his footsteps on the porch, wondering why he chose to work late instead of coming home to her, all had combined to make her realize she would never be enough for her husband. And she'd rather be alone than not be enough.

After her shower she dressed quickly, able to hear Gideon's and Colleen's voices mingling with Sam's and drifting up the stairs from the kitchen. Once dressed, she descended the stairs, trying to control the butterflies in her tummy. She walked into the kitchen and flashed a nervous smile. "Good morning," she greeted her sister- and brother-in-law.

"Thanks," she said to Sam as he thrust a mug of coffee into her hands. She sat down at the table and cupped her hands around the mug, the warmth soothing on her icy fingers.

"So, 003, are you ready for this big adventure?" Colleen asked.

"Double-o-three?"

Colleen nodded. "I figure you're 003 and I'm 004. Between the two of us, hopefully we'll be on par with 007 and manage to get the bad guys."

Julianne laughed, some of her tension ebbing a bit. "So, what's our game plan?"

It was nearly two hours later when Julianne and Colleen drove toward Baker Enterprises, Gideon following behind them in a van. As a private eye, Gideon had been a godsend in working up a plan that would hopefully keep Julianne and Colleen safe. Julianne was wired and Gideon would be monitoring the equipment from the corporation parking lot.

"You nervous?" she asked Colleen as she parked her car behind the enormous glass-and-steel structure that housed Baker Enterprises.

"Terrified," Colleen admitted with a tense smile.

"Me, too." Julianne shut off the car engine. "But I would have been even more terrified if I had to do this alone." She reached over the seat and touched her sister-in-law's arm. "I can't thank you enough."

Colleen held up her hands. "Stop, no more of that talk. We're family. We do whatever it takes to help each other."

Family. Family for now, Julianne thought. If this worked and Sam was no longer in danger of being arrested, they would be family no more.

Shoving this thought out of her mind, she concentrated on the task at hand. Just before she and Colleen entered the back doors of the building, she looked back into the parking lot, comforted by the sight of Gideon's van. He'd assured them that if he heard any indication of trouble, he would enter the building with guns blazing to insure their safety.

Their first stop was into Barry's office, where they found him, feet up on his desk and munching a glazed donut. "Hey, what a surprise." His feet hit the floor and he placed the remaining piece of donut on his desk. He hugged both of them, then gestured for them to sit in the chairs in front of his desk. "So, what brings two of the lovely Baker women to see me?"

"Something strange has happened," Julianne explained. "We weren't sure who to talk to about it, but we thought we could trust you."

"Of course you can trust me," Barry said, a frown creasing his forehead. "What's happened?"

Julianne opened her purse and took out the two charms. "I received these in the mail on Saturday with a note from Sam. He said one is his and the other belonged to Colleen. He said they were vitally important to clearing his name."

Barry looked at Colleen. "How did Sam get yours?"

Colleen shrugged. "I don't know. I'd thought I'd lost mine. I wore it out about a month ago, then put it in my jewelry box. When Julianne called me to tell me about all this, I checked, and mine was missing."

Barry reached for the charms, but Julianne quickly tucked them away in her purse. She wondered if the confusion he radiated was real or if he was a skilled actor already plotting how to get the charms from her.

"I don't understand. How could a couple pieces of jewelry be important to Sam's defense?"

"We were hoping you'd know something about it," Colleen said.

"Where were they mailed from?" Barry asked, a frown of perplexity wrinkling his brow.

"Casey's Corners, Kansas," Julianne answered.

"His other sisters live out there, don't they?"

Colleen nodded. "Carolyn and Bonnie. Their charms were stolen a couple of weeks ago."

"What we want to know is what we should do with the charms?" Julianne said, pulling the conversation back to the most pertinent issue at hand. "They must be important for Sam to risk getting them to me for safekeeping. What do you think we should do?"

Barry held out his hands in a gesture of helplessness. "I don't know what to tell you. If Sam thinks they are important, then they must be. I suppose you should take them home and put them in a safe place."

That was the advice they got from each and every person they spoke to whom Sam thought might be in a position to carry out a money-laundering and murder scheme. It took them nearly two hours to talk to everyone, then they headed back to Julianne's home, Gideon following in the nondescript van.

A few minutes later they were all seated around the table as Julianne and Colleen told Sam about their various meetings. "Garrison was the last person we spoke to," she said.

"How did he react?" Sam leaned forward, the lines of his face taut with strain.

Julianne stifled the impulse to lean forward, caress the stress away. She hated seeing him like this, coiled so tight, almost haggard with strain. Oh, Sam, this has to work, she thought.

She shrugged. "Just like everyone else. He was confused and bewildered. He said he couldn't imagine how the charms could play a part in any of this and why you'd think them important enough to send to me. He suggested we put them in a safe place."

"We talked to all the people in prominent positions at the company and that was the reaction we got from all of them," Colleen added.

For a moment they were all silent, disappointment hanging heavy in the air. "Anyone hungry?" Julianne finally asked, needing something to do, something to occupy her thoughts and energy.

"I'm not hungry," Sam replied, his discouragement deepening his tone.

"Nothing for me," Gideon said.

"Me, neither," Colleen agreed.

Julianne sighed and looked at the others. "So, what do we do now?"

"We wait," Gideon replied.

* * *

The afternoon hours moved slowly, filled with frayed nerves and anxiety. Colleen and Gideon played two-player card games while Julianne and Sam took turns wearing out the carpet with their pacing.

Despite her preoccupation with the charms, Julianne couldn't help but notice the obvious affection between her sister- and brother-in-law. They spoke to each other wordlessly, with secret gazes and furtive touching.

Julianne tried to remember a time when she and Sam had done the same thing, felt so attuned with each other they didn't need words, felt such passion they couldn't help but touch each other as many times as possible.

Yes, she and Sam had once had that. Like a flower planted in fertile soil, their love had initially bloomed full and healthy. But, like all living things, it had needed nourishment and instead they had let it die from neglect. Was it her fault? She didn't know anymore, couldn't get the proper objectivity to be able to claim part of the fault as hers. All she knew was the sadness of loss, the emptiness of broken promises and unfulfilled dreams.

"Juli?" Sam's voice pulled her out of her thoughts, back to the present. "You all right?"

She nodded and sank down onto the sofa. "This waiting is making me crazy."

Sam sat down next to her, his arm going around her in an effort to comfort. "Unfortunately, there's nothing that says this scheme is going to work."

Julianne took his hand in hers and squeezed it. "It's got to work, Sam," she whispered fervently.

He was silent for a moment. "If it doesn't work, I'm going to turn myself in." He stilled her protest with a shake of his head. "I can't allow this to go on any longer. We've had to send Emily away from home. You're a nervous wreck, and I love you both too much to allow this to go on any longer."

Before Julianne had a chance to answer, the doorbell rang. They all froze. Julianne shot a look of sheer panic at Sam, who smiled in encouragement. "You can do this," he whispered. He stood. "Just act natural and remember we're all listening from the kitchen."

By the time the doorbell rang again, Julianne was alone in the living room, the other three hidden in the kitchen. She raced her hands nervously down the sides of her slacks, afraid to answer the door, afraid not to.

"Barry." She greeted Sam's friend in surprise. Barry? Please don't let it be Barry, she thought as he stepped into the foyer. Barry was Sam's best friend. They'd gone to school together. Barry had been Sam's best man at their wedding. He'd been her friend, too. "What are you doing here?"

"Julianne, I've been thinking about those charms all afternoon. I don't think it's a good idea for you to keep them here."

"What do you think I should do with them?" she asked softly, wondering how a man could pretend so well. Was any amount of money worth this kind of betrayal? She wanted to scream at him, pound her fists against his chest. If what she suspected was true, he was here to get the charms, which meant he was involved in the death of Sam's father. He'd stolen Joseph's life, destroyed Sam's, and affected hers so profoundly nothing would ever be the same again.

"Julianne, if Sam said those charms are important, then they are. Somebody got in here the other night to let off a smoke bomb. What's to stop someone from coming in to steal those charms?"

"So, what should I do?" Julianne asked again.

Barry raked a hand through his sandy hair and expelled a deep sigh. "Shoot, I don't know. Maybe you should take them to the bank and put them in a safe-deposit box. I just couldn't go home without telling you I think you need to do something to make sure they're safe." He leaned over and kissed her on the forehead, then stepped back toward the front door. "Just make sure you keep them where nobody else will be able to find them."

Julianne watched as he walked down the driveway and got back into his car. She closed the door and leaned heavily against it, the adrenaline that had shot through her moments before now gone.

"You okay?" Sam entered the foyer, followed closely behind by Gideon and Colleen.

"Yes, but I don't think Barry is who we're after." She rubbed the center of her forehead tiredly. "I looked into his eyes. I didn't see deception."

"Surely if he's the one we're after he would have offered to take the charms for safekeeping," Colleen added. "Surely he would have tried to get them from you."

Julianne nodded and allowed Sam to pull her close against his chest. "I was so afraid it was him." She looked up at her husband, the man she would always love with all her heart. Even if she left him, even if they were no longer married, Sam would always own a very large part of her soul. "I knew if it was Barry it would break your heart."

Sam smiled down at her. "There's only one person in this world who could truly break my heart."

His words stabbed into Julianne. She didn't want to hurt Sam, but she couldn't go on living a life of hurt herself.

"Anyone want coffee?" she asked as she moved out of Sam's arms.

They had just sat down at the kitchen table when the doorbell rang once again.

Julianne's gaze shot to Sam, and he felt her dread. He gave her a reassuring nod, then moved to just inside the kitchen door so he could hear what was happening.

Garrison Fielder's voice filled the hall, and suddenly Sam knew. Of course it was Garrison. It made sense. Garrison who knew the company inside out, who had always made it his business to know everything about everyone. Garrison, who had friends on the fire department, friends on the police force. Sam's father had always told Garrison everything. Hell, he'd probably told Garrison about the code on the charms.

Sam clenched his fists tightly at his sides, wondering how he could have been such a fool. Why hadn't he realized before that Garrison was the logical person responsible for all of it...the money-laundering, his father's death...everything.

He focused his attention on the conversation taking place between Julianne and the older man.

"My dear, I've stewed about those charms all afternoon. I'm very concerned about Emily's and your safety."

"No need for you to be concerned," Julianne replied. "I'm going to take the charms and put them in a bank safe-deposit box in the morning."

"Why don't you let me take care of that for you?" Garrison's voice was smooth, filled with fatherly consideration as Julianne led him into the living room.

"Really, I can handle it. I'll just stop at the bank on my way to work in the morning," Julianne said.

"I'm afraid I really must insist, my dear." The elderly man's voice held an underlying tone of steel. "Where are the charms, Julianne?"

Sam indicated for Colleen and Gideon to remain in the kitchen as he crept out into the hallway, needing to be close enough to circumvent any danger directed at Julianne.

"Garrison, really, it's fine. The charms are in a safe place for the night," Julianne protested, tension thick in her voice.

"Julianne, you don't understand. I need those charms and I don't intend to leave here without them."

Sam stepped into the doorway of the living room. "Why do you need them, Garrison?"

"Ah, the prodigal husband has returned." A smile of bemusement lit Garrison's features. "I knew you were here. I set that smoke bomb hoping to smoke you out into the open. It worked. I watched as you carried your daughter out of the house." He sighed impatiently as Julianne gasped. "You know why I need those charms. I need to erase the files your father left, files I imagine are rather incriminating."

Sam took a step toward the older man, his hands once again fisted as he fought to control an enormous rage. "You killed my father."

The smile fell from Garrison's face. "Sam, that was an accident. I didn't mean for Joseph to get hurt." A frown of frustration furrowed his brow.

"He accused me of being responsible for the money-laundering, said he was going to turn me in. I pleaded with him, tried to reason with him, told him I'd make sure the operation stopped, but he wouldn't listen."

"And so you shot him," Sam accused.

"No. I drew the gun so he would listen. I just wanted to scare him a little, buy some time so I could make him understand that I'd clean things up. There was no need to go to the authorities. When he saw the gun he went crazy, charged me...I...the gun went off...I never meant to kill him."

"Oh, Garrison." Disappointment and grief weighed heavily in Julianne's voice.

"Garrison, it's over," Sam said, moving to stand next to his wife.

"I don't think so." Garrison pulled a gun from his coat pocket and focused it on the two of them. "I don't want any more bloodshed, but I do need those charms."

"Oh, Garrison, what am I supposed to tell Emily?" Julianne asked, her voice barely a whisper. "She adores her Uncle Garri and Aunt Letta."

"Letta has nothing to do with this. She doesn't know anything." For the first time emotion rang in his voice and the gun wavered in his hand.

Sam seized the moment and threw himself forward, hitting the old man in the chest and tumbling them both backward. As the gun skittered across the floor, Sam was vaguely aware of Julianne screaming and Colleen's and Gideon's footsteps as they raced into the room.

He grunted as Garrison grabbed him around the neck, his strength deceptive with his age and appearance. Sam managed to break his hold, furniture thrown askew as they rolled, each one trying to gain an advantage on the other.

Garrison fought for his life, and each punch, each kick came from the strength of that survivalist instinct. But self-righteous rage filled Sam, the rage of a man whose father had been murdered, whose life had been torn asunder.

He finally managed to gain the upper hand and delivered a resounding uppercut to Garrison's jaw. Garrison's head slammed against the floor and he remained unmoving, although conscious. "It's over," Sam repeated as he straightened.

"I called the police. They should be here any minute," Gideon said, then looked disdainfully at Garrison. "I, too, have friends on the force. Honest friends."

Garrison sat up, a hand rubbing his jaw. "They'll never believe you," he said to Sam. "It will be your word against mine. Of course, your wife and your other relatives would lie for you."

"True, but we have an ace in the hole," Gideon explained. He pulled a small tape recorder from his pocket. "Did anyone ever tell you that you talk too much?"

At that moment the sounds of sirens rent the air and within minutes the house swarmed with police officers. Both Sam and Garrison were arrested and taken to the station where it took hours to straighten out exactly who was guilty of what.

Sam finally emerged with a tired but victorious smile on his face. He embraced Julianne, his arms holding her tightly, as if he'd never again let her go. "It's finally over," he said as he released her.

"Garrison?"

"He's in there spilling his guts about everything. Seems he likes the horses and got in over his head with gambling debts. The people he owed money to came up with the plan to launder through the corporation. The police are thrilled, Garrison is giving them names, dates and evidence incriminating people they've been trying to arrest for a long time."

"And the charms?"

"Confiscated by the police. They'll check out the computer file and use whatever information is there, although the way Garrison is talking, they won't need anything else."

"And you have your life back," Julianne said softly.

"We have our lives back," he said, then, throwing his arm around her shoulders, they left the police station and headed for their car.

Julianne knew she should tell him. He deserved to know that she didn't intend to spend the rest of her life with him. She slid onto the passenger seat and leaned her head back against the headrest. Closing her eyes, she searched for the right words.

As he got into the car, his energy filled the interior. Exuberant joy radiated from him, a thrill of life renewed, a future left to live. "We've got to call Carolyn and get Emily home as soon as possible," he said, his voice filled with such spirit it only made Julianne's heart ache more.

She opened her eyes and looked at him, saw the sparkle back in his eyes, the despair gone beneath a euphoric happiness. "Oh, Juli, there's so much to be done, so many months to make up for." He started the car. "There was a time when I wasn't sure everything would ever straighten out, but now I feel like I've been granted a new life." He frowned thoughtfully. "I'm going to have to sit down and have a long talk with my sisters. We're going to have to completely restructure the corporation. Garrison wasn't the only one working there who was crooked. We'll need to do a complete housecleaning."

Julianne tensed. Of course one of his first thoughts would be the business. Always the business. Restructuring the corporation would take time. Nothing had changed. Nothing was ever going to change. And Julianne knew she wasn't willing to settle for life with Sam anymore. It hurt too much. She drew in a deep breath. "Sam, I want a divorce."

Chapter Ten

With a squeal of the brakes, Sam pulled over to the curb. He turned and stared at her in shock. "Is this some kind of a joke?" he asked.

"I wish it were," she answered, not able to meet his eyes, not wanting to see what emotions her words had placed there.

"But, Juli...after all we've been through?" He continued to stare at her incredulously.

"Sam, nothing we've been through has fixed what was wrong with our marriage to begin with." She finally got the courage to meet his gaze. "I didn't make any promises, Sam. You knew this was a possibility."

"But you slept with me. We made love. I thought that meant everything was okay."

Julianne sighed. She should have realized that's what he would think. Whenever they'd had a fight, Sam had always thought making love would solve the problems, make her forget her unhappiness. And it did, for the brief moments he held her in his arms. But when it was over she was left with an emptiness as aching as ever.

"Sam, making love didn't fix things, it can't fix things. Sex has always been wonderful between us. It was never the problem."

"Then what is the problem?" he asked, his voice deepening in anger. "What do you want from me, Julianne? What can I do to make things right? Do you want me to quit my job? Devote myself to spending every hour of every day with you?"

Julianne flushed. "That's not fair, Sam. Of course I don't want you to quit your job." She sighed in frustration. "Why does it have to be all or nothing with you?" She drew in a deep, weary breath. "It's too late. You can't make things right. It's just too late." She slumped back against the seat and stared unseeing out the passenger window.

Sam restarted the engine and pulled away from the curb, heading toward home. Not home, Julianne thought. Not her home anymore. She closed her eyes, the hot press of tears burning them. She knew she had made the right decision, but that didn't make it hurt less.

She could tell Sam was angry by the way he drove. Usually a smooth, flawless driver, he now jerked the car, braking harder than necessary as his hands tightly clenched the steering wheel.

Eventually the anger would dissipate and Julianne thought he'd probably be relieved. No longer would he feel torn between his work and her. Never again would he have to face her anger or disappointment when he worked long into the night, forgetting family functions and plans previously made. Yes, sooner or later he'd be relieved that she was gone, and he no longer had to worry about her.

And eventually she would stop wondering why she hadn't been enough, why he seemed to take such pleasure in work, and so little in time spent with her.

Hopefully they could emerge from their marriage as friends. It was important for Emily's sake. Julianne didn't want the little girl torn apart by her parents' adult problems.

Sam didn't speak for the remainder of the ride home and when they got into the house, he disappeared into the guest bedroom. Julianne knew he would deal with whatever he was feeling as he always had...alone.

She went into the bedroom she'd shared with her husband for eight years. As she changed into her pajamas, her mind raced, trying to figure out what her next course of action should be.

Climbing into bed, she realized she hadn't thought much further than telling Sam her intention of divorcing him. She hadn't thought about contacting a lawyer, where she would eventually live, or none of the other specifics. Lying on her back, staring at the dark ceiling, she also realized she was simply too exhausted to think. She'd figure it all out in the morning.

Sam stared at the wall in the spare room, but the pale ivory wallpaper held no answers to the questions that plagued him. He'd thought when he finally cleared his name the pieces of his life would fall back into place. Instead he felt his life shattering into a million pieces.

"Sam, I want a divorce."

Julianne's words haunted him, angered him, and ultimately filled him with a deep sadness. There had been a strength in her words, a steely resolve that made him realize her mind was made up and nothing he did or said would change it. She was really leaving him, and he didn't know how to stop her.

He rolled over and stared at the ceiling until dawn crept in, chasing away the night shadows and filling the room with golden hues. Still no answers came.

At seven he finally got up and showered, then went down to the kitchen to make coffee, hopeful that he and Julianne could rationally discuss things this morning. Last night she'd been exhausted, having ridden a roller-coaster ride of emotions. Perhaps her mindset would be different this morning. Perhaps she would give him one more chance.

As he walked into the kitchen his heart fell to his feet. Julianne was already there, sipping a cup of coffee at the table, a suitcase next to her side. "Going somewhere?" he asked as he poured himself some coffee.

She nodded. "I'm going out to Carolyn's for a while."

He sank down across from her, searching her face for some sign of weakness, hoping to see doubt, indecision, but there was none. "How long is 'a while'?"

"I'm not sure." She stared down into her mug. "I need some time to think, to figure out what I want to do, where I go from here."

"Julianne, I..." He paused as she held up a hand to silence him.

"Please, Sam. Please don't make this more difficult than it is." Suppressed tears made her voice fuller, deeper than usual. "I just can't live with you anymore. It hurts too much." She finished her coffee and stood up. "I've got to go. My plane leaves in two hours." She picked up her suitcase and started for the door, then hesitated and turned back to him, her eyes shining with the burden of tears. "Do me a favor, Sam? Don't marry again

without warning your prospective wife that all she
can ever hope for is stolen moments in the middle
of the night when you're too tired to be at the office. Make sure she understands how driven you
are.'' She hesitated another moment, then sighed.
''I just wish I could understand.''

Before he could answer, she was gone. He remained at the table for a long time, emotion roil-
ing inside him until he felt seasick from the turmoil.
Gone. She was gone, leaving behind only a lingering scent of her perfume.

He hadn't thought she'd really leave; had honestly believed she'd back down after a good night's
sleep. He rubbed a hand over his face, wondering
how he'd managed to lose the person most important to him. He didn't know how to be different,
didn't know how to change to please her.

Finishing his coffee, he thought about Julianne's parting words. Driven? Yes, he was driven
to succeed in the corporation. What was wrong
with ambition? What was wrong with seeking success? Certainly sacrifices had to be made, but he
realized now he'd sacrificed too much. And now it
was too late to go back and undo the damage.

He could have made more promises, sworn he'd
always be home for dinner from now on, but he
knew eventually he'd break those promises. Because she was right, he was driven. And God help
him, he didn't know why or how to fix it.

The house resounded its emptiness, a hollow echo of nothing that tore at his heart. He couldn't stand it. He had to get out of here.

Moments later, his car automatically headed in the direction of the corporation, he kept his thoughts carefully schooled from his personal problems. Instead he focused on what had to be done to fix the internal management problems of the company.

He walked into the building and cheers immediately resounded from the people he'd worked with for years. The sound filled his chest, but couldn't penetrate the pain in his heart left by Julianne's leaving. He quieted the group, said a few words of thanks and encouragement, then headed for his office.

When he reached his office door, he walked by, on impulse heading for the office that had belonged to his father. "Martha," he greeted the gray-haired secretary with an affectionate hug.

"Oh, Sam, it's so good to have you back," the older woman exclaimed, dabbing the tears at the corners of her eyes. "Nothing has been the same around here what with your father and you gone."

He gestured toward the inner office door. "Is anyone in there?" he asked.

She shook her head. "Hasn't been anyone in there for months, not since we cleared out Mr. Baker's paperwork." Again tears glistened in her eyes. "I still can't believe he's gone. I keep waiting for him to walk through that door and tell me I need to take dictation.''

Sam gave her shoulder a sympathetic squeeze. ''I'll be in there for a few minutes. I'd rather not be disturbed.''

Martha nodded and went back to her desk as Sam entered the private office that had belonged to his father.

Taking a seat behind the large oak desk, Sam looked around, surprised the office looked just like it always had. In the four months he'd been gone, other than general cleaning, nobody seemed to have touched anything.

It was the office of a businessman, with little personal flavor at all. No pictures of family, no favorite knickknacks, nothing to indicate a life other than business.

Sam leaned back in the plush chair and closed his eyes, his thoughts consumed with the man who'd been his father. Joseph Baker had been a dynamic businessman, a strong leader, and a lousy father. A grunt of surprise escaped Sam at this thought and yet he knew it was the truth. Any relationship Sam had gained with his father had been garnered when Sam joined the business.

Memories he hadn't thought about for years tumbled inside his head. And in those memories he found not only his father's flaws, but his own, as well.

He sat forward and buried his head in his arms, tears burning as he tried to suppress their descent. No use. As he thought about a life, a future without his Juli, sobs choked him and, in a final surrender to grief, Sam allowed himself to cry.

He didn't know how long he sat there. Once the tears were gone, anger began to build. His eyes flew open and he shoved the chair back from the desk. He'd never been a quitter, and he'd be damned if he became one now. He wasn't about to let Julianne walk out of his life without one hell of a fight. Besides, he knew now. Knew what drove him. And, if nothing else, Julianne deserved an answer to that question.

In three long strides he was out of the office and standing next to Martha's desk. "Martha, would you please call the airlines and get me on the next flight to Casey's Corners, Kansas?"

"Certainly." She picked up the phone.

"I'll be back in ten minutes," Sam said, leaving her to make the necessary arrangements.

He raced toward the security office, where he found Barry sitting in his office reading the morning paper. "I pay you an astronomical salary so you can read the paper?" Sam said as he entered the office.

"Sam." Barry jumped up and the two men embraced. "It's good to have you back."

"I'm leaving again in just a few minutes, but I didn't want to go without telling you how much I

appreciate everything you did for Julianne and
Emily while I was gone.''

Barry waved his hands in dismissal. ''That's what
friends are for,'' he said. ''Where are you off to
now? I'd think there would be a million things for
you to take care of with all the arrests I heard went
on last night.''

''There are a million things to do, but they can
wait. Julianne flew out this morning to spend some
time with Carolyn.'' Sam swallowed hard, then
continued. ''She wants a divorce, Barry.''

Barry winced. ''Yeah, I gathered things were not
well between the two of you.''

''Things haven't been well for a very long time,''
Sam admitted, not only to his friend, but to himself. ''I've been a fool, and it's time I make some
changes. I just hope it really isn't too late.''

An hour later Sam sat on a plane carrying him to
Casey's Corners, Kansas. His heart pounded with
anxiety as he willed the plane to go faster. He closed
his eyes, hoping he was not too late.

''Can I get you anything?'' A flight attendant
shoving a drink cart down the center aisle smiled
pertly.

''No, thanks.'' Sam returned her smile, then
leaned his head back once again. The only thing he
needed, the only thing he wanted, was for Julianne
to give him one final chance.

* * *

"I promised Emily and the twins a trip to the park today. Want to come?" Carolyn asked Julianne.

"If you don't mind, I'd rather just stick around here. I'm fighting off a headache," Julianne replied. "Probably didn't get enough sleep last night."

Carolyn nodded. "From what you told me, you had quite a night." Carolyn smiled sympathetically. "Aspirins are in the cabinet above the sink in the kitchen if you need them. We'll probably be gone for a couple of hours. When the twins get into the sandbox, it's hard to drag them away."

"Emily, you be good for your Aunt Carolyn," Julianne instructed her daughter, who at the moment was rolling a ball back and forth between the twin two-year-old boys.

"Aunt Carolyn says I'm a good helper," Emily proclaimed proudly.

"Indeed you are," Carolyn agreed. "She's been a very good helper in the last couple of days. And with these two I can use all the help I can get." Carolyn smiled at her adopted boys, her eyes filled with motherly love. "Well, gang. Let's get a move on. The sandbox awaits."

Within minutes Carolyn and the children were gone, leaving Julianne alone in the silence of the house. She went to the kitchen and got the bottle of aspirin, wondering if they could cure her heartache as well as the pounding of her head.

She hadn't expected her decision to leave Sam to hurt quite as badly as it did. Although there was a part of her relieved that the final decision had been made, the relief wasn't yet strong enough to mask the pain.

She hadn't told Carolyn much, just that she and Sam were having problems and she needed some time to get her head together. She'd been grateful that Carolyn hadn't pried, but instead offered her the warmth and support of her home for as long as necessary.

Swallowing two aspirins, Julianne wondered when the heartache stopped. How long did it take to put a man and a marriage in the past? How long before she stopped looking backward and began moving into the uncertainty of a new future? She stared out into the backyard, knowing that no matter how much time passed, her heart would always bear the scars of loving Sam Baker.

"Juli."

At the sound of the familiar voice, she gasped and whirled around.

"Sam. What are you doing here?" Her heart thundered in her chest. She didn't want to see him, didn't feel strong enough to talk to him. She wanted it ended. Over.

"I have to talk to you."

She wrapped her arms around herself, drawing on the inner strength that had seen her through the months he'd been gone. "We have nothing to talk about." She sank down at the table, her gaze averted from him.

He scooted into the chair across from her. "Juli, please look at me, listen to me. Don't shut me out."

"Don't shut you out?" She did look at him, shocked at the raw emotion emanating from his eyes. "You've shut me out for years, Sam." She sighed wearily. "We've led separate lives for a very long time. I've just decided it's time to make it legal."

"Juli, I don't want a divorce," Sam replied softly.

"And I can't live any longer on empty promises."

"I know." He folded his hands on the top of the table, his gaze lingering on hers. "What about some explanations?"

"Explanations?" Despite her desire not to talk to him, not to be sucked back into the mess they'd called a marriage, she was intrigued. "What kind of explanations?"

"After you left this morning I went to the company, but instead of going into my own office, I went into my father's. I sat there and thought back, back to the childhood I told you was happy and normal, and I realized I'd not only lied to you, but I had been lying to myself."

"I don't understand."

Sam raked a hand through his hair and drew in a deep breath. "You know what I remember most about growing up? Loneliness. After my mother died, I was sent to prep schools and rarely saw or heard from my father."

Julianne heard the deep emotion in his voice and it sent a shudder of shock waves through her. She'd never seen Sam with emotions out of control, but at the moment he seemed to be fighting a losing battle for some modicum of composure.

Still, she kept hold of her heart, afraid to hope anything would ever change and absolutely refusing to consider the possibility of going back to where they'd been.

"My dad had nothing to do with me until I joined the business. And for the first time I knew what it was like to have a father, to feel like I had some worth, to belong." He looked back at her, the blue of his eyes intensified by the sheen of tears. "Juli...I've worked long hours, spent as little time with you and Emily as possible because I've been so afraid."

"Afraid?" she asked softly, unsure what to make of this vulnerable, hurting man in front of her.

He nodded and looked down at his hands. "Afraid that if I spent too much time with you, you'd realize I was a nothing, a nobody. When I wasn't at the office, I was afraid I'd go back to being that invisible little boy nobody seemed to want."

"Oh, Sam." Despite her resolve to be strong, in spite of her intentions not to be taken in by false promises and empty apologies, she had no defense against this.

She'd been so afraid it was her fault he'd overworked, had been so afraid he didn't love her enough to want to spend time with her. She now realized he loved her so much he was afraid to spend time with her, afraid of not living up to the man he wanted to be.

"When I was on the run, sleeping in alleys, camping out beneath bridges, it wasn't thoughts of my desk or my office that kept me going, kept me sane." He looked at her again, his eyes brimming with love. "It was thoughts of you, Juli. You were my strength and my hope."

He stood and moved across the room, then burrowed his face in his hands. "I've been such a fool, such a stupid, crazy fool. I've been somehow trying to prove myself to my father, to myself, and instead, alienated you. I don't know how it got all messed up. All I know is I want you back in my life, Julianne." He pulled his hands down and looked at her once again. "I want to fulfill those dreams of yours, I want to share your days and nights, listen to your thoughts and plan our future together. No more broken promises or missed picnics. Just tell me you'll give me one more chance."

Julianne stumbled from her chair, tears blurring her vision as she reached out to him. He pulled her against his chest, his heart thundering in the same rhythm of her own . . . the rhythm of love.

"Oh, Sam, I've never been very strong where you are concerned," she finally said. "I want to scream at you, I want to be angry with you, but I can't."

He looked down at her. "Does this mean you'll give me a chance to be the husband you want? The kind of husband you deserve?"

She nodded, her heart too full to speak. His lips claimed hers in a sweet, tender kiss that was filled with the taste of a new beginning and a glorious future.

"Daddy!" Emily's excited squeal interrupted their kiss. As they broke apart, Emily launched herself at Sam.

"Hi, sweetcakes," he greeted her, swinging her up onto his hip.

"Daddy, I'm so happy," Emily exclaimed.

"You are? And what has you so happy?" Sam asked.

She put her arms around his neck and laid her cheek against his. "You're here and it's daytime and you aren't a ghost daddy anymore, are you?"

"No, Emily, I'm not a ghost daddy anymore. And I'm never going to be a ghost daddy again." He looked at Julianne, his eyes so blue, so filled with love, it stole her breath away. "I intend to be the best daddy and the best husband in the whole world. We're going to have lots of tea parties, and picnics and special time together from now on."

"I love you, Daddy," Emily said.

Sam closed his eyes and squeezed Emily tight. "I love you, too."

She wiggled impatiently. "I gotta go now, Daddy. Aunt Carolyn is waiting for me in the front yard. We're gonna spray the sand off the twins." Like a tiny whirlwind, she blew out the door.

"Juli?" He motioned her back into his arms. "What do you say we get married again...do the renewing vows thing?"

"Are you serious?" She looked up at him, touched and thrilled at the thought of marrying him all over again.

"I think we should. It will be a new start, a fresh beginning."

She snuggled close to him, wondering how she ever imagined she could live without him. "I think it's a wonderful idea."

"Juli...you promise when the preacher asks if you'll take me as your husband, you'll say 'I do'?"

She grinned teasingly, knowing her love for him was there in her eyes, radiating to him. "Gosh, Sam, I can't make any promises."

He growled and nuzzled her neck. "Don't tease me, Julianne."

She sobered and took his face in her hands.
"Sam, I love you. I'd be happy to marry you
again."

"Oh, Juli, and I love you." His mouth descended to claim hers in a kiss that pledged a lifetime of love. As his lips sweetly caressed hers,
Julianne knew the rest of her life would be spent
loving Sam.

Epilogue

For the first time in years, all the Baker brood were gathered together. The police had finally released the charms, and the family had come together at Sam's house to pull up the mysterious computer program that Joseph had created before his death. While the adults sat in the living room, the children played in the kitchen, their laughter filling the house with joy.

Later that afternoon Sam and Julianne were renewing their vows in the same church where they had married eight years ago. As Julianne watched her husband feed in the secret codes from the back of the charms, she marveled at the changes that had taken place over the past month.

Sam seemed to have finally found peace with himself and was no longer driven by the demons of work. He put in eight-hour days and was always home by dinnertime. Julianne had resumed her work at the day care and enjoyed sharing the details of her day with Sam over dinner.

They had grown from the people they had been before, taking pleasure in time spent together, new intimacies explored, sharing private pieces of each other without fear. It had been a magical time, a good basis for a life-long marriage.

"I'm in," Sam said, pulling Julianne's thoughts to the present. Colleen, Bonnie and Carolyn all crowded around Sam as the file appeared on the screen and Sam hit the print button on the printer. As the printer whirred out a copy, Sam frowned. "This doesn't look like any kind of incriminating evidence," he said thoughtfully.

"What is it?" Beau, Carolyn's husband asked, moving to stand behind his wife.

"It looks like it's a letter...a letter to all of us," Sam replied.

The printer stopped, and Sam picked up the hard copy as everyone else found seats around the living room. Julianne remained at Sam's side, her hand on his shoulder in a gesture of support.

"Read it, Sam," Bonnie said impatiently.

He nodded and cleared his throat. Julianne squeezed his shoulder, sensing his emotions rising to the surface.

"'My dear children,'" he began. "'If you are reading this, then I must be gone. I've had a sense for the past weeks of time running out, and as I face the possibility of death, I find myself looking back over my life.'" Sam cleared his throat once again, obviously emotional. "'I am saddened to discover I am a man who's led a relatively empty life. When your mother died, leaving behind the four of you, I was filled with fear at the daunting task of raising you. I knew mergers and bottom lines. I didn't know children and emotional needs. I thought by not parenting and leaving the parenting to house-keepers and good schools, I couldn't make a mistake. I was wrong.'"

Sam paused a moment to draw in a deep breath. "'I made my mistakes through love, for none of you should ever doubt that I love you. And my wish for you all is to find love and be happy. If the corporation becomes a chain around your necks, sell it. Don't make the mistakes I did. Find and surround yourself with love. Have children and surround them with love. For in the end, that's what is important.'" Sam folded the paper, indicating that was the end of their father's message to them all.

"He wasn't a bad man," Carolyn said softly. "Just a frightened man." Her husband Beau pulled her close.

Sam nodded, and Julianne knew he was thinking of his own fears, fears that had nearly destroyed their marriage. "How ironic that the file that broke the entire case was simply a letter from a father to the four of his children," he observed.

"A letter we all needed to hear," Colleen said. She reached for Gideon's hand. "Hearing Dad's words has filled up a hole in me I didn't realize I had. Although in my heart I always knew Father loved us all, I didn't realize until now how much I needed to hear his love in words."

"Me, too," Bonnie agreed, leaning against her husband Russ.

Sam smiled at his sisters, then threw an arm around Julianne's shoulders. "But Dad must have done something very right for all of us. We've come through a hard time, and we've managed to fulfill his final wish." He looked at Carolyn and Beau, Bonnie and Russ, Colleen and Gideon, and finally to Julianne. "We've all found love, have surrounded ourselves with it. We've learned what's important, and it's right here in this room. Family... and love."

"Hey, speaking of love, don't we have a wedding to attend?" Bonnie quipped.

Julianne smiled at her sisters- and brothers-in-law. "Since we're all here, why don't we make it a quadruple ceremony? All the Baker brood renewing their vows in honor of Joseph?"

"I think that's a great idea," Sam said as the others agreed.

"However," Julianne cautioned them, "I don't intend to share my second honeymoon with the entire Baker brood."

They all laughed and in their laughter Julianne heard the sounds of healing, of forgiveness, and most of all, love.

* * * * *

COMING NEXT MONTH

Conveniently Wed: Six wonderful stories about couples who say "I do"—and *then* fall in love!

#1162 DADDY DOWN THE AISLE—Donna Clayton
Fabulous Fathers
Jonas's young nephew was certainly a challenge for this new father figure. But an even bigger challenge was the lovely woman helping with the little tyke—the woman who had become this daddy's wife in name only.

#1163 FOR BETTER, FOR BABY—Sandra Steffen
Bundles of Joy
A night of passion with an irresistible bachelor left Kimberly expecting nothing—except a baby! The dad-to-be proposed a *convenient* marriage, but a marriage of love was better for baby—and Mom!

#1164 MAKE-BELIEVE BRIDE—Alaina Hawthorne
Amber was sure the man she loved didn't even know she existed—until the handsome executive made a startling proposal, to be his make-believe bride!

#1165 TEMPORARY HUSBAND—Val Whisenand
Wade's pretty ex-wife had amnesia—and forgot they were divorced! It was up to *him* to refresh her memory—but did he really want to?

#1166 UNDERCOVER HONEYMOON—Laura Anthony
Pretending to be Mrs. "Nick" Nickerson was just part of Michelle's undercover assignment at the Triple Fork ranch. But could she keep her "wifely" feelings for her handsome "husband" undercover, too?

#1167 THE MARRIAGE CONTRACT—Cathy Forsythe
Darci would marry—temporarily—if it meant keeping her family business. But living with her sexy cowboy of a groom made Darci wish their marriage contract was forever binding....

Conveniently Wed

"I do," the bride and groom said...without love
they wed—or so they thought!

Don't miss these six irresistible novels about tying the
knot—and *then* falling in love!

Coming in July, only from

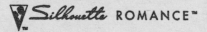 *Silhouette* ROMANCE™

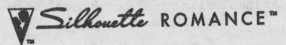

This July, watch for the delivery of...

An exciting new miniseries that appears in a different Silhouette series each month. It's about love, marriage—and Daddy's unexpected need for a baby carriage!

Daddy Knows Last unites five of your favorite authors as they weave five connected stories about baby fever in New Hope, Texas.

- **THE BABY NOTION** by Dixie Browning
  (SD#1011, 7/96)

- **BABY IN A BASKET** by Helen R. Myers
  (SR#1169, 8/96)

- **MARRIED...WITH TWINS!**
  by Jennifer Mikels
  (SSE#1054, 9/96)

- **HOW TO HOOK A HUSBAND (AND A BABY)**
  by Carolyn Zane
  (YT#29, 10/96)

- **DISCOVERED: DADDY** by Marilyn Pappano
  (IM#746, 11/96)

Daddy Knows Last arrives in July...only from

DKLT

SILHOUETTE... Where Passion Lives

Add these Silhouette favorites to your collection today!

Now you can receive a discount by ordering two or more titles!

SD#05819	WILD MIDNIGHT by Ann Major	$2.99	☐
SD#05878	THE UNFORGIVING BRIDE by Joan Johnston	$2.99 u.s. ☐ $3.50 can. ☐	
IM#07568	MIRANDA'S VIKING by Maggie Shayne	$3.50	☐
SSE#09896	SWEETBRIAR SUMMIT by Christine Rimmer	$3.50 u.s. ☐ $3.99 can. ☐	
SSE#09944	A ROSE AND A WEDDING VOW by Andrea Edwards	$3.75 u.s. ☐ $4.25 can. ☐	
SR#19002	A FATHER'S PROMISE by Helen R. Myers	$2.75	☐

(limited quantities available on certain titles)

TOTAL AMOUNT	$_____
DEDUCT: 10% DISCOUNT FOR 2+ BOOKS	$_____
POSTAGE & HANDLING	$_____
($1.00 for one book, 50¢ for each additional)	
APPLICABLE TAXES**	$_____
TOTAL PAYABLE	$_____
(check or money order—please do not send cash)	

To order, send the completed form with your name, address, zip or postal code, along with a check or money order for the total above, payable to Silhouette Books, to: **In the U.S.:** 3010 Walden Avenue, P.O. Box 9077, Buffalo, NY 14269-9077; **In Canada:** P.O. Box 636, Fort Erie, Ontario, L2A 5X3.

Name:_____

Address:_____ City:_____

State/Prov.:_____ Zip/Postal Code:_____

**New York residents remit applicable sales taxes.
   Canadian residents remit applicable GST and provincial taxes.

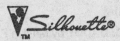

Silhouette®

SBACK-JA2

THIS CONFIRMED BACHELOR
IS ABOUT TO BECOME ONE OF OUR

DADDY DOWN THE AISLE
by
DONNA CLAYTON
(SR #1162)

Jonas Winslow was determined to keep his orphaned nephew—but the child's aunt, Robin Hampstead, loved the boy as if he were her own! The solution: a *temporary* marriage. Until Jonas began seeing this lovely woman in a new light—and wished they could live as husband and wife in every sense of word!

"I do," the bride and groom said…without love they wed—or so this *Fabulous Father* thought!

Don't miss **DADDY DOWN THE AISLE**
by Donna Clayton, part of the Conveniently Wed
promotion, coming in July, only from

Silhouette
R O M A N C E™

FF796